'Let's make sure everyone believes that we are on a date, OK? And try and look happy about it. A lot of women would pay to be in your shoes.'

'I'm not a lot of women.'

He'd gathered that. 'Then you'll have to fake it. Let's go.' Glancing at his watch, he gestured to her bag. 'Leave that. I'll get someone to take it out of here.'

'Give me five minutes. I need make-up. And shoes, for that matter.' She leant down to pull out a silver clutch bag and a pair of shoes. Long, elegant feet slipped into lime-green high-heeled wedge sandals and his pulse kicked up a notch.

Enough. Straightening up, she pivoted to face the mirror, leaving him with an alluring view of her bare back, the black dress tapering down in a V to the voluptuous curve of her bottom.

Adam forced himself to turn away.

'I'm ready.'

He swivelled round and a whoosh of air was expelled from his lungs as desire upped another notch. In a few minutes she'd been transformed from au naturel beauty to glamorous allure. Which meant she had him coming and going.

Her hazel eyes shimmered and her lips were outlined in glossy dark red. Lips he wanted to claim right here. Right now. *Oh, hell.* He was screwed; no way was his libido leaving this party.

Dear Reader

This book is incredibly special to me—partly because it is my Mills & Boon debut, but also because I am so excited that Olivia and Adam, who lived inside my head for a long time, have made it into the big wide world.

The first chapter of this book wrote itself—I knew that nothing would stop Olivia from getting to Adam once she had him in her sights. I also knew that Adam would put up the fight of his life to avoid being bagged.

But there the book stopped. Until one day not so long ago when Olivia and Adam demanded I get them out of the ladies' restroom and let them try and sort out what happened next…

So I did!

I hope you enjoy reading about the trials and tribulations that beset them on their sometimes rocky path to love.

Nina xx

HOW TO BAG
A BILLIONAIRE

BY
NINA MILNE

© 2014 Nina Milne

ISBN: 978-0-263-24279-9

Nina Milne has always dreamt of writing for Mills & Boon®—ever since as a child she discovered stacks of Mills & Boon® books 'hidden' in the airing cupboard. She graduated from playing libraries to reading the books, and has now realised her dream of writing them.

Along the way she found a happy-ever-after of her own, accumulating a superhero of a husband, three gorgeous children, a cat with character and a real library... Well, lots of bookshelves.

Before achieving her dream of working from home creating happy-ever-afters whilst studiously avoiding any form of actual housework, Nina put in time as both an accountant and a recruitment consultant. She figures the lack of romance in her previous jobs is now balancing out.

After a childhood spent in Peterlee (UK), Rye (USA), Winchester (UK) and Paris (France), Nina now lives in Brighton (UK), and has vowed never to move again!! Unless, of course, she runs out of bookshelves. Though there is always the airing cupboard...

HOW TO BAG A BILLIONAIRE
is Nina Milne's debut for Modern Tempted™!

This title is also available in ebook format
from www.millsandboon.co.uk

For my husband, Sandy, and our children,
Jack, Harmony and Harry.
Thank you for putting up with me whilst I wrote this book.
It probably wasn't easy.

PROLOGUE

August edition. Glossip *magazine*

Today's advice column is for all you gold-diggers out there.

How to bag a billionaire in six easy steps.

Looking for a lifestyle change?

Down on your luck?

Don't despair! How about you bag yourself a billionaire?

OK, ladies—here's how you do it:

1. Identify your target:

He needs to be loaded and he needs to be single—and wouldn't it be a bonus if he were drop-dead gorgeous, as well? Too much to hope for? Not today. Because we have done some digging and found a dream target for you. Drumroll, please... We give you Mr Adam Masterson, Founder and CEO of Masterson Hotels. Richer than rich and sexier than sin.

2. Discover what he likes in a woman:

We've done some research and it wasn't easy, folks. Adam Masterson is a bit of a dark horse. But the good news is that over the past years he has been seen about town with a variety of types. Blonde or dark. Small or tall... This field is open to all. Adam Masterson's only criteria is beauty: the man likes his ladies easy on the eye.

3. Adjust yourself accordingly:

Hubble, bubble, toil and trouble... Lotions, potions, get on with the motions! Start beautifying, ladies.

4. Work out your target's routine:

This is a tough one. Adam Masterson has no routine— Paris one day, London the next. But we have it on good authority that his swish flagship hotel might be the place to start.

5. Waylay target:

Time to find your inner minx and cook up some schemes.

6. Seduce target:

Over to you...

Adam Masterson is out there. He is worth billions and he is worth bagging. Who will bag him first?
Happy Hunting!

CHAPTER ONE

SHE COULD GET arrested for this.

The thought pounded her temples as Olivia Evans glanced around the dark and thankfully deserted London alleyway at the back of Masterson Mayfair, the flagship of Masterson Enterprises hotel portfolio.

Why had she thought gatecrashing one of London's most exclusive parties was a good idea?

A bead of perspiration prickled her forehead. Swiping it away with an impatient gesture, she pressed her lips together hard. This was a good idea because it was the only idea left. It was imperative that she see Adam Masterson before he gallivanted off on yet another business trip. She had tried every conventional method of contacting him, but the man was more closely guarded than the president of the United States. There was every possibility his PA doubled as Head of National Security.

Desperate times called for desperate measures; hence Operation Break and Enter.

Olivia hauled in a breath; with any luck that would push the panic down. One final glance around and, standing on her tote bag, she applied herself to the task of picking the window lock. Amazing how some childhood skills didn't desert you. Even those learnt from one of the more unsavoury of her mother's boyfriends. The thought of her mother had her shoving the hooked pick deeper into the lock until she felt it butt into the mechanism; she would not give up now.

Nerves knotted inside her before giving way to a buzz of exhilarated relief as the lock gave. Pocketing the pick, she pulled the window open, then jumped off the tote bag. She thrust the bag through the gap a minute later.

So far, so good. Her reconnaissance of the hotel had been spot-on; the room she had chosen as an access point was a small conference room which wouldn't be in use tonight as the hotel was being exclusively given over to a charity gala. Hosted by Adam Masterson. *Finally* she had him in her sights.

She scrambled up onto the window ledge and her nerves retied themselves right back up. What her recon *hadn't* bargained for was the size of the window gap.

Logic. Angles. Weight. Mass distribution. Those were the things to focus on—because, come hell or high water, Olivia *would* get inside. Never mind that it looked to be physically impossible.

So should she wriggle in forwards on her tummy or try to get in backwards? There were so many things that could go wrong: she could get stuck, she could fall into the arms of a waiting security guard... Maybe this wasn't such a brilliant idea.

But if she gave up now then she wouldn't get a chance to talk to Adam Masterson.

That was unacceptable.

Good thing she was flexible.

Adam Masterson perched on the edge of his security officer's desk and scowled at the CCTV footage of the woman balanced on the windowsill.

What the hell was she doing? Apart from an excellent impersonation of Catwoman. Dressed completely in black, with a beanie pulled low over her forehead, it was impossible even to know her hair colour.

More to the point, who the hell was she? Journalist? Photographer? Wishful thinking… He'd already arranged publicity for the event. Which meant here was yet *another* hopeful player in the new party game Bag a Billionaire. Bad enough that he knew the ballroom would soon be awash with legitimate guests scheming how to waylay him over the canapés. At least they'd paid for the privilege, with the money going to a more than worthy cause.

Tendrils of memory threatened and he cut them off before they could take hold. He'd had his daily surfeit of grim memories already today, following his earlier conversation with his ex-wife and the news that she was remarrying. He was happy for Charlotte, but the exchange had brought back recollections of a time in his life he was less than proud of. *Way* less.

Plus, it had highlighted the way their lives had gone in the eight years since their disastrous union. There was Charlotte, with the happy-ever-after she had always wanted; here was Adam, being pursued by a bunch of women mining for his gold.

Speaking of which, right now he had to contend with his gatecrasher. He bit back an exasperated groan; he didn't need this. The entire billionaire-bagging thing was getting old.

'Do you want us to apprehend her?' Nathan asked.

Adam pulled himself into the present and focused on the screen. The woman appeared to be engaged in some sort of internal Q and A session before she wriggled limbo-dancer-like through the gap in the window.

An arrow of desire shot straight through him.

He ran a hand over the top of his head. Talk about misplaced. A probable stalker, a definite intruder, was breaking into his hotel and his libido had decided to come to the party. The woman landed on the floor, glanced round the empty room and opened the bag she had pushed through earlier.

Adam opened his mouth to instruct his security chief to get a team down there.

And closed it again on a strangled gargle, unable to wrench his eyes from the screen as the woman pulled the black beanie from her head and shook out a mane of extraordinary hair. Strawberry blonde tresses, with the balance towards strawberry, fell past her shoulders.

Crossing her arms, she hoisted her black jumper over her head to reveal a white tunic top, and then with a little twist pushed her jeans down her hips.

Misplaced or not, desire pulled his libido's strings. Time to get a grip; better yet, maybe it was time to get a date. Clearly it had been too long—ever since that article had appeared and the baggers had emerged from the woodwork he'd put himself on a stint of enforced celibacy. Partly because the thought of being chased for his money brought a tang of distaste, and partly because he wanted any press attention to be focused on his charitable activities and not his bedroom ones.

Until now it hadn't been an issue.

'So what next?' Nathan asked.

It was a good question.

The woman was now fully clothed in an outfit that at a glance resembled the uniform worn by all hotel employees; she'd obviously done her research. White tunic top, black trousers—she'd even got a clipboard. The intent look on her face backed up the determined set of her jaw as she swept her magnificent hair into an efficient bun.

Picking up the bag, she opened the door and walked down the corridor. Her stride confident, she looked as though she knew exactly where she was going and why.

Of course there was no way he would allow her access to his guests; it was just fascinating to watch her at work. The first bagger to catch his interest and certainly the most resourceful.

But enough was enough. Time to mobilise the troops.

Before he could say anything Nathan's massive body tensed as she ducked into the ladies' restroom. 'Better hope she *is* a bagger. For all we know she could be building a bomb in there.'

Staring at the screen, Adam concentrated on unclenching his jaw. It was an outside chance, but it was still possible that the intruder was armed. And he had let a moment of inappropriate attraction blindside him. A pulse started to beat in his cheek and he closed his eyes, grounded himself, before pushing himself away from the desk in a single lithe movement.

'Close the ladies'. Be discreet. Say it's a plumbing problem and send your men down there in cleaners' uniforms.'

Nathan nodded. 'I'll go in and get her out,' he said.

Adam shook his head. 'I screwed up. I'll go in.'

'But…'

'No buts,' Adam said. 'We could've stopped her by now. That was my call and I didn't make it.' Too busy stewing over the past whilst lusting over a stranger. Who said men couldn't multitask?

'I still think…'

Adam shook his head. If he didn't sort this one out himself the strawberry blondee stranger would haunt his dreams for too long. Best to make her real. Expose her as the avaricious gold-digger she undoubtedly was whilst avoiding the baggers no doubt waiting to hunt him down in the ballroom.

He picked up his tux jacket and gave Nathan his best impression of an action hero. 'I'm going in.'

* * *

Olivia mentally ran through her entire and extensive repertoire of swear words. This was ridiculous! This was supposed to be the easy bit. The bit where she locked herself into a cubicle and transformed herself from faux hotel employee to fake ballroom guest. All she had to do was change into a party dress. Good grief! What sort of personal shopper couldn't get herself into a dress? A dress she'd tried on at home with no problem.

But now the stupid zip on the stupid little black blend-right-in dress was stuck. Worse, she couldn't get out of the skintight concoction to *un*stick it.

As she twisted she lost her balance and the back of her knee thunked the lip of the toilet seat. 'Ouch!' Biting her lip, she stilled. Please let there be no one out there. Though…surely there *should* be someone out there? Guests must have arrived in droves by now so it made sense that someone would want to freshen up in the ladies' restroom.

That was the essence of the last stage of her plan. Guests would only be allowed entry into the hotel on production of an invitation, embossed and coded and impossible to duplicate. This was a private party, an annual gala that raised hundreds of thousands of pounds for Support Myeloma, thanks to the auctioneering powers of Adam Masterson. But she was already in the building, and as the invitations were inspected at the foyer of the hotel Olivia figured she should be safe.

Particularly as the plan was to leave the ladies' with a group of other women who would serve as camouflage. Then she would find a large potted palm and lurk unnoticed until the moment arrived when she could snag Adam Masterson.

After all, she was good at lurking at parties.

Memories skittered through her brain as echoes of raucous laughter peppered with the pop of champagne corks reverberated in her eardrums. How she had hated the numerous shindigs her mother had hosted, even as she'd understood Jodie Evans's desperate need to extract fun out of every second of a life that had stacked the odds against her. Olivia hadn't begrudged her mother one of those seconds of fun; she had wished with all her heart for Jodie to be happy. The knowledge that she could never repay everything she owed her mum was always with her.

Closing her eyes, she sucked air into her lungs. For goodness' sake! This was not the time for a trip down memory lane. Any minute now someone was bound to come in here so she had better hurry up. How hard could this be? She was *flexible*, remember? She reached round for the zip.

'Need a hand?'

Olivia froze as an unmistakably male voice drawled out the question.

In slow motion she forced herself to look up at the man observing her over the top of the cubicle. He must be standing on the toilet in the next door cubicle, her brain told her dully, trying to operate past the volcano of panic about to erupt in her chest.

Dark hair, light brown eyes, square jaw, a nose that was ever so slightly off-shape… Recognition slammed her like a sucker punch. 'It's you,' she breathed.

His eyebrows pulled together in a deep frown as his lips tightened. 'In the flesh,' he said.

Olivia opened her mouth but the words evaporated under the heat of his gaze. Plus, she was damned if she knew the best way to explain her presence. Blurting out her reason for being there whilst standing half-dressed in a toilet cubicle had *not* been part of the Masterson Master Plan.

Still, she was going to have to work with what she had; this was an opportunity. 'Mr Masterson,' she began. 'I can expl—'

'I need to check your bag,' he broke in.

'My bag?'

'Yes, your bag,' he said, his impatience tingeing the air.

Olivia glanced down at the bag in confusion. Looking back up at the exasperation that lit the brown eyes, she realised his motivation was irrelevant. Right now it seemed clear he wouldn't listen to anything she said until she gave it to him. She ducked down awkwardly and picked up the bag.

'I'll come round,' he said.

She heard the thud as he presumably jumped down from the toilet; she pushed the door open and held out the bag. 'Look, is this really necessary?' she asked, a shudder of aversion shivering through her as he started to sift through the contents.

'Yes,' he stated. 'My security chief is worried that you are locked in here constructing a bomb.'

Fabulous! Her stomach plummeted into a free fall of panic; she was under suspicion of being a terrorist.

Come on, Olivia. Calm down. You've talked your way out of worse than this before.

Though she suspected that talking her way past this man would be akin to melting iron with an incense stick.

Still, she had to try. She took a step forward out of the cubicle and straightened her spine.

'I realise all this is a bit bizarre, but I'm not a terrorist and I'm not here with the intention of hurting anyone. If—'

Adam Masterson wasn't so much as looking at her, let alone listening. Instead he was on the phone.

'Nate,' he said. 'I've checked the bag. Our enterprising intruder locked herself in the toilet to get dressed, not to build a bomb.' He listened for a moment and then put the phone back into his pocket.

OK. At least the terrorist theory had been knocked on the head. Not that Adam Masterson looked relieved; if anything the set of his lips was even grimmer, the frown deeper. Time to try again.

'Look, I'm truly sorry,' she said. 'I never meant to cause so much hassle. I really, *really* just want to—'

A derisive snort interrupted her. 'I know what you really, *really* want to do, and I'm really, *really* not interested.'

Olivia frowned. 'You can't possibly know why I'm here.' She was having trouble enough believing it herself.

Adam pulled his phone out of his pocket.

'Hang on!' Olivia said. 'You've got to listen.'

He shook his head. 'Nope, I don't. I've got to get Security in here to remove you from the premises.'

The panic erupted in her chest; this was her chance and she'd blown it. Unless… Maybe now was the time to utilise her black belt in taekwondo.

Propelled by the sheer impossibility of failure, Olivia launched herself at him.

'What the—?'

Taking advantage of his millisecond of surprise, she knocked the phone from his hand.

To no avail.

In a fluid movement he'd caught the mobile and shock juddered Olivia's body as she collided with an immovable wall of chest. Strong arms locked behind her back in a hold way too powerful for her to break even as she leant back, shoving her palms flat against his chest.

Her breath escaped in short, sharp pants as she looked up at him. For a fleeting second his light brown eyes darkened and focused on her lips. Unable to help herself, she dropped her gaze to his mouth as a sudden shiver prickled her skin.

A shiver not of fear but of desire.

Which was ridiculous. Right now her instincts should have kicked in; she should be at least attempting to struggle free. Instead she couldn't stop staring at the mesmerising shape of those firm, capable lips. His heart pounded under her hand; her fingers curled into the silk of his white shirt.

As she pressed her own lips together to moisten them something primal flickered in his eyes. His arms tensed to pull her forward. Then abruptly he released her.

Her skin tingled where his arms had touched her and Olivia stepped backwards, until the cold marble of the counter pressed into the backs of her thighs. Her heart thumped painfully against her ribcage. Perspective—she desperately needed to locate some. Along with control. Her master plan was in tatters and somehow she had to salvage it. Before Adam Masterson called Security.

He stood there, those gorgeous lips set in a grim line. Anger darkened his face; his eyes were cold chips of mud. 'Lady, just how far are you prepared to go to bag me?'

'Excuse me?' What was he talking about? Perhaps his proximity had addled her brain cells completely. Somehow she had to pull herself together and try and turn this situation around. She had no idea what had happened in those charged seconds in his arms but she couldn't let it ruin everything. 'I don't understand.'

An exasperated sigh hit the air. 'Drop the act. I know you're here to "bag me",' he said, hooking his fingers in the air to indicate quotation marks.

'As in murder you and put you in a body bag? Tempting, but given your security levels I'll pass.'

For a second she thought she saw his lips give the tiniest of quirks. Was it possible the man possessed a sense of humour?

He swiped his hand over his mouth and shook his head. 'You haven't heard of Bag a Billionaire?' The narrowed eyes, the creased forehead were both clear indicators of patent disbelief; the gleam of humour had obviously been a mirage.

'Nope. Honest.'

His frown deepened. 'In a nutshell, some idiot magazine reporter wrote an article advising wannabe gold-diggers on how to bag themselves a billionaire and identified me as the target. Since then I've arrived home to find a naked woman in my bed with "Kiss me Quick, Kiss me Slow" tattooed on her stomach and an arrow pointing downward, my mail yesterday included some rather explicit photographs, I have had women break the heels of their shoes and collapse in a heap in front of me, and women's cars seem to miraculously break down wherever I go.' Pausing, he eyed her. 'I'm sure you get the picture.'

'That's terrible,' Olivia said. 'But...'

'Terrible?' he echoed, the mocking note jarring through the air. 'I agree. Though I must say no one has resorted to gatecrashing a party with quite such style as you have.'

It took a minute for the implications of his words to sink in before outrage smacked her mouth wide open. 'You think... You mean... You think I'm like one of those women?'

He leant back against the wall, arms folded. 'You've broken into my hotel and thrown yourself into my arms in a dress that is conveniently falling off you—what do you expect me to think?'

Anger started to bubble at his sheer arrogance, stirred frothier by the small part of her that conceded the devil had a point.

One hand slammed on her hip even as the other held the dress up. 'I admit I've broken into your hotel, but I did not *throw myself* at you. I promise you I haven't risked arrest for the supposed pleasure of "bagging" you.'

For a moment he studied her face and she met his gaze full-on, saw something flicker in the milk chocolate depths. She prayed he could hear the truth in her voice. Otherwise he would have her marched out of here any second now and she couldn't let that happen. There was way too much at stake here—and not just for herself.

'Please,' she said. 'I understand why you are suspicious but you don't need to be. I promise. Give me a chance to prove it to you. Hear me out. Please.'

'Fine,' he said. 'You've got ten seconds.'

CHAPTER TWO

HARD TO TELL who was more surprised—the strawberry blonde stranger or himself. Irritation coursed through his veins; he'd been blindsided by a beautiful face and a spectacular body. This woman was bad news, and no matter what lies she was about to spin from that gorgeous mouth the key point was that they *would* be lies—a calculated strategy with the aim of locating his wallet.

The chances of her not being a billionaire-bagger were minuscule, yet there had been a vibrancy to her voice, a desperate glint in those hazel eyes that had clouded his usually impeccable judgement.

Pushing the sleeve of his tux jacket up, he looked at his watch. 'Five seconds left. Four...three...'

'My mother is pregnant,' she blurted out.

Her words echoed around the bathroom and bounced off the mirrored tiles.

What on earth did she expect him to do? Maybe she *wasn't* a billionaire-bagger. Maybe she was crazy. 'Offer her my congratulations,' he said. 'And now I think it's time for you to go.'

'I need to tell you who the father is.'

Adam gusted out a sigh. 'Lady, if you think you can scam me into believing it's me that's *not* going to fly.'

For a start his unwanted intruder had to be in her mid-twenties, and he hadn't dated an older woman in a very long time. But even if that weren't the case Adam always made 100 per cent sure that pregnancy was an impossibility. One thing was certain in his life: he was not father material. After all, he was a Masterson through and through and he knew his own limitations. The less than stellar circumstances of his marriage had showcased his shortcomings all too brightly.

'I'm not trying to scam anyone.' Her hands twisted into the folds of her black dress. 'The baby's father is *your* father. Zebediah Masterson. And I need to find him.'

Long practice at the poker table kept his face neutral even as her words travelled towards him in slow motion, each one slamming into him with the force of a sucker punch.

Come on, Adam. Keep cool. This was nothing more than an über-clever scam, a fantastic concoction woven to get his attention.

'Rubbish,' he stated.

'It's not rubbish.' One slim hand rose to jab the air in emphasis; her other hand still held the black dress up. 'Or rocket science. It's simple biology. My mum is pregnant and Zebediah is the father. So I need to find him.'

Moisture prickled his temple with foreboding before common sense reasserted itself. No way would Zeb want a replay of fatherhood. Plus, surely even Zeb would have bothered to get in touch over something like this?

'I don't think so,' he said.

'And *I* don't think you get it. I need to find him because I need to tell him about the baby. He doesn't know.'

For a treacherous second relief ran through his veins; if this preposterous tale was true at least Zeb hadn't deliberately walked away from another unwanted baby. The way he'd walked out on Adam. *Whoa.* This wasn't about the past; it was about the here and now and this no doubt mythical baby.

'I see,' he said, allowing scepticism to load each syllable. 'How convenient for you.'

Hazel eyes narrowed. 'There is nothing convenient about this. Have you any idea how difficult it is to locate your father? I've spent weeks looking for him and finally I discovered *you*. So if you could just tell me how to contact him I'll be on my way.'

Was she serious? 'Not happening.'

Brows just a shade darker than her hair arched. 'Why not?

'Because I don't want you harassing my father with some trumped-up paternity suit.'

'Trumped-up paternity suit?' Her free hand clenched into a fist and he braced himself. 'Why are you assuming it's trumped-up? For—'

The buzz of his phone cut off whatever else she had been about to say. He pressed it his ear and Nate's voice erupted.

'What's going on in there? Guests are arriving thick and fast and they are getting more and more curious.'

'The intruder isn't a threat.' Or at least not to the guests; she was having a less than happy effect on him. 'I'll be there in a minute.' Once he'd decided what to do about Little Miss Minx and her preposterous claim. In the meantime, with any luck, his guests' curiosity might divert them from the billionaire-bagging hunt.

Dropping the phone back into his pocket, he studied her. Hmm… He drummed his fingers on his thigh as he went through the options, a glimmer of a possibility sparking.

'You can't just go,' she said. 'I need to know where to find your dad.'

'No.' Adam considered his idea from all angles. 'Turn around.'

'What?' Bewilderment layered her voice

'Turn around. I'll zip the dress up for you.' He tipped his palms into the air. 'You're going to the ball.'

It was the perfect solution. She remained where he could see her until he could disprove her story. And, as the icing on the cake, if he turned up to the ball with a beautiful woman on his arm he'd have a shield against all the other billionaire-baggers. Win-win. Adam made no effort to conceal the smirk that touched his lips.

There was a moment's silence as her jaw dropped. 'Don't be ridiculous.'

'I'm not being ridiculous. You strike me as a loose cannon. So until I understand the situation you will stay glued to my side.'

The words triggered an unwanted reaction: the thought of how she had felt in his arms earlier made his fingers itch to pull her right back to him. Madness, and yet she was the epitome of allure. The expressive hazel eyes, the delicate elven features and luscious mouth combined to make her ludicrously kissable.

Throw in hair the colour of sunset and a body that showcased curves in all the right places and he was in trouble.

His fingers tingled. *Hell.* All of him tingled and any desire to smirk left him.

Great. His libido had decided to overlook the fact that this woman was an adversary, only here as a player in an elaborate scheme. Though unlike the other baggers it could be that her plan was to forgo the billionaire and aim straight for the money. Use Zeb to get to the cash. His expression hardened. No way was that happening—and she'd seriously underestimated him if she thought it was.

'I have no intention of being glued to your side.' Pushing herself off the sink, she glared at him. 'And I am not coming to the ball. It doesn't even make sense.'

'It makes perfect sense to me. You could go to the press.

You could disappear and resume your quest for Zeb. You know what? I have no idea what kooky scheme you may come up with.'

'I wouldn't go to the press! *Why* would I do that?'

'Publicity? Money? Fun? I don't know.' Raking a hand through his hair, he stepped forward. 'Why would you break into my hotel to gatecrash my party? It's hardly the mark of a sane woman.'

'It's the mark of a desperate woman.' Anger sparked the hazel of her eyes with green flecks. 'Funnily enough breaking and entering wasn't my number one choice. I tried to get hold of you by more conventional methods but your PA wouldn't let me near you and you ignored my letters,' she continued. 'Presumably I fell into the probable billionaire-bagger category.'

'Honey, you *still* fall into that category.' And he'd better not forget it. Glancing at his watch, he muttered a curse. 'We can discuss all this later. Right now you are coming with me.'

'Says who? You can't force me to go with you.'

'Want to bet?' Adam took another step forward. 'Here's your choice. You can put your shoes on and accept my kind invitation or I will call the police and have you charged with breaking and entering. Your call.'

Her whole body vibrated in sheer disbelief. 'That's blackmail!'

'Breaking and entering is a criminal offence,' he returned.

'I had a good reason.'

'So do I. So, prison or party? Your choice.'

Her lush lips pressed together as she stared at him before hitching slim shoulders. 'Fine. I'll come to the party. But you have to promise me that afterwards you will give me your father's contact details.'

Unease solidified in his gut; there was no hint of insincerity in her voice. In fact if push came to shove he would swear she didn't want to come to the party at all.

'After the party we talk,' he said. Given twenty minutes, he had no doubt he could rip her story to shreds.

'Fine,' she agreed, and reached round to tug at the zip on her dress once more.

'Let me do that.'

For a moment he thought she'd refuse, but instead she gave another little shrug and spun around to place one palm flat on the marble counter, strawberry head bowed as though she didn't wish to see his or her reflection in the mirror.

Probably a good thing. Because confronted with the smooth expanse of her back his lungs constricted and heat tingled on his cheekbones.

It's only a back, Adam.

Yet his fingers trembled as he reached out and inadvertently brushed the base of her spine as he tugged at the zip.

'It's stuck,' he said, the words straining past the breath of disproportionate desire that had hitched in his throat.

'I know that.' The snap of her words was insufficient to drown her audible gulp; the small shiver that caressed her skin in goosebumps testified to the effect of his touch. 'I told you that I wasn't deliberately falling out of it.'

With relief he freed the silken material and whooshed the zip up, the noise vying with the pounding in his ears

'So how will you explain who I am?' she demanded as she turned to face him.

'I've been thinking about that.'

'Oh, goodie,' she said. 'Care to share?'

His lips twisted with the irony of his idea. 'Congratulations! You've bagged a billionaire.'

Her body froze into utter immobility before she shook her head. 'I am *not* coming as your billionaire-bagger date.'

Adam frowned; behind the anger in her eyes was a vulnerable gleam of genuine horror.

'No way am I walking in there with everyone believing I'm with you for your money. I'd *rather* go to prison.'

'Don't be melodramatic. Who cares what people think?' Adam lifted his shoulders in pure indifference.

'In this case, me,' she said, as her hands slammed on the curve of her hips.

Irritation coursed through his veins at the continued sheer sincerity of her tone and the fact that he couldn't work her out.

'Tough,' he said. 'You're coming to the ball—and what's more you're coming as my date. I'd rather people assume you've bagged me than work out why you are claiming to be here. I do *not* want any publicity about this.'

'What happened to not caring about what people think?'

'Honey, I don't care what people think about *you*. I *do* care what they think about my dad. And right now I don't need the publicity backlash.' Not when he was hosting the gala tonight and launching another charity event the next evening. 'The press are already having a field day with the bagger theme.' Amazing how many women were willing to bare their bodies and perjure their souls by lying to the tabloids.

Resolve hardened in him. No way was all the hard work and effort he had put into the Support Myeloma charity going to waste. Not one copper penny should be diverted from the cause he championed in his mother's memory. An image of his mother sprang to mind: pale and weak, but still with the beautiful smile that would stay with him for eternity. Those last words of love: 'You brought me joy, baby. Remember that. Be happy. I love you.'

Adam blinked away the memory as a small assessing frown creased the brow of his new date for the night. 'So no matter what happens the press are not getting their grubby paws on this trumped-up story of yours.'

His words were calculated to annoy her; a riled adversary was far more likely to slip up. 'It is *not* trumped-up,' she said, the words hissing through gritted teeth,

Adam shrugged. 'The papers won't care whether it is or not; they will still have a good old grub around. Your life and your mother's life will be taken apart with a fine toothcomb.'

Her skin paled and wariness entered her hazel eyes. 'I don't want publicity, either. I just want to find your father. That's all.'

'I get that. But right now I have a charity ball to host and a reporter out there who will be very interested in who you are. So you are coming as my date.'

She expelled a gusty sigh. 'Fine.'

Anyone would think he'd asked her to hook up with the devil himself. 'It won't kill you. You may even have fun.'

'Yeah, right. Somehow I doubt that.'

Affront touched his chest. *Grow up, Adam.* Why did he care that she seemed so anti the whole idea of being with him? 'Then you need to pretend. I want to make sure all the other billionaire-baggers out there believe I'm bagged for the night.'

Her mouth smacked open. 'This gets better and better. So this isn't just for the reporter, or to keep me in sight. You're going to use me as *protection*. Big, strong man like you?'

'Size and strength aren't much use against a pack of scavenging gold-diggers.' He shrugged. 'I'll use what it takes. Hey, I've got no issues with using a beautiful woman as a shield.'

Her dark eyebrows rose. 'And if I *wasn't* beautiful?' she asked, and he could almost see icicles form around each word.

'Then it wouldn't work,'

Disdain flashed from her hazel eyes and desire tugged in his groin. Standing there in the simple elegant black dress, she looked magnificent.

'The magazine article specified that only beautiful women should enter the arena,' he explained.

His words did nothing to mollify her. 'No doubt based on your past dating career?'

'Most of my dates *are* beautiful,' he agreed. 'I'm not going to apologise for that.' Yet his conscience gave a sudden inexplicable twang. 'So let's make sure everyone believes that we are on a date, OK? And try and look happy about it. A lot of women would pay to be in your shoes.'

'I'm not a lot of women.'

He'd gathered. 'Then you'll have to fake it. Let's go.' Glancing at his watch, he gestured to her bag. 'Leave that. I'll get someone to take it out of here.'

'Give me five minutes. I need make-up. And shoes, for that matter.' She leant down to pull out a silver clutch bag and a pair of shoes. Long, elegant feet slipped into lime-green high-heeled wedge sandals and his pulse kicked up a notch.

Enough.

Straightening up, she pivoted to face the mirror, leaving him with the alluring view of her bare back. The black dress tapered down in a V to the voluptuous curve of her bottom.

Adam forced himself to turn away and pulled his phone out of his pocket. Time to alert Nathan as to what was going on and make sure any evidence of this bathroom caper was hidden from the no doubt goggling eyes and flapping ears of guests and reporters alike.

'I'm ready.'

He swivelled round and a whoosh of air was expelled from his lungs as his desire upped another degree. In a few minutes she'd transformed from au naturel beauty to glamorous allure. Which meant she had him coming and going.

Her hazel eyes shimmered and her lips were outlined in glossy dark red. Lips he wanted to claim right here. Right now. He was screwed; no way was his libido leaving this party.

CHAPTER THREE

PANIC SHEENED THE BACK of Olivia's neck as they approached the imposing ballroom door. This *so* hadn't been the plan. The plan had been more of a sidle into the ballroom, not a grand entrance. The plan certainly hadn't included snagging the role of Adam's billionaire-bagger date.

A woman only interested in the balance of his bank account... Olivia bit her lip. Fantastic. Here she was, playing the role she had always abhorred. Judging a man by wallet size had been her mother's gig.

Olivia had hated it. Hated that her mother was the quintessential gold-digger even whilst she'd known Jodie was looking out for the two of them the best way she could. Thrown out by her family, pregnant at sixteen, Jodie had used what she had. Her looks and her limitless sex appeal. Both of which had garnered her a more than respectable income and a less than respectable lifestyle.

'Hey. You still with me?'

The deep voice tinged with concern rescued her from Memory Lane and snapped her to the here and now. To the opulent room with its fluted pillars and glittering glass chandeliers. To the noise of laughter, the pop of champagne corks and the clink of crystal, all indicating the guests were having a good time.

Enough. Shaking off the past, she relegated it to where

it belonged. The past couldn't be changed. But the present and the future…? They were firmly in her control.

So it was time to locate her backbone. All Olivia had to do was allow the world to believe her to be a billionaire-bagger in order to discover the whereabouts of Zeb Masterson. Then her unborn brother or sister would have a dad. A proper father. The kind of dad that Olivia had yearned for so desperately: a dad who acknowledged his child and wanted to be part of her life.

'I'm right here,' she said, with a clench of her nails into her palm to ground herself.

'Then do you think you could smile?'

'I'm not a smiley person.'

'Well, it may be time to cultivate the art. Reporter at six o'clock and heading our way.'

He slid an arm around her waist and Olivia bit back a gasp, trying to ignore the snap, crackle and pop of desire that ignited in her at his touch. Instead she focused her attention on the blonde woman headed towards them with curiosity written all over her face.

'We'd quite given up on you.' The reporter put a hand on Adam's arm. 'Plus, we've all been dying to know who your mystery guest is. So introduce me.'

There was a heartbeat of silence.

Oh, hell.

Adam didn't know her name.

The reporter raised perfectly threaded blonde eyebrows.

Olivia opened her mouth just as Adam's hand tightened round her waist, twisting her body slightly so that she instinctively looked up at him. Not even a glint of alarm flickered in the brown eyes; instead liquid copper warmth melted over her. Her throat felt parched; he was gazing at her as though he couldn't keep his hands off her, as if names were a mere bagatelle.

Then he smiled—the kind of smile that had her toes

curling around the edge of her lime-green sandals. 'Sweet-heart, this is Helen Kendersen, columnist from *Frisson* magazine.' He turned his gaze to the reporter. 'And this, Helen, is my nomination for *Frisson*'s Most Beautiful Woman of the Year award.'

His arm pushed into the small of her back and she stepped forward, holding her hand out. 'Olivia Evans,' she managed.

'So, how do you feel about having bagged yourself a billionaire for the night?' The reporter's voice was light, almost jokey, but her blue eyes were alert as she waited for an answer.

Olivia knew she should answer in kind—should have found time in the unprecedented disaster of this evening to prepare a witty, sophisticated comeback. But her brain refused to co-operate. Instead humiliation flushed her cheeks.

She heard a low laugh coming from her left and knew the question had been overheard.

Memories crowded her brain. There she was in the play-ground, surrounded by the pigtail brigade with their shiny shoes and perfectly packed lunches. *'My mum says your mum is a tramp and you'll be exactly the same.'* Noses in the air, holier than holy. *'So I'm not allowed to play with you.'* The chant taken up as they circled her. *'Tramp, tramp, tramp...'*

Her hands balled into fists at her sides; if only the solu-tion now was as easy as it had been all those years ago. Un-fortunately punching Helen Kendersen on the nose wasn't an option. Even more regrettably, her mind still hadn't formulated a single witty rejoinder. The only words com-ing to mind and being transmitted to the tip of her tongue were wildly inappropriate.

She sensed Adam's head turn and looked up to see his brown eyes rest on her face with an expression she couldn't interpret. His arm moved from her waist to drape around her shoulders, the soft fabric of his tux brushing her suddenly sensitised skin. The gesture was totally, unexpectedly protective.

'Wrong call, Helen,' he said, his voice pleasant but with an impossible to miss steely undertone. 'Credit me with a bit more sense. Olivia is not a billionaire-bagger; she is a bona fide date.'

A sudden warmth touched Olivia's chest. Was Adam defending her? She wasn't sure. It could be that he simply thought the assertion would definitively shield him from the baggers in the room. Whatever his reasons, he'd given Helen Kendersen pause.

The blue eyes sharpened. 'Well, colour me surprised,' she said. 'Especially as I can't remember you ever bringing a *date*, bona fide or not, to this event. And here was me assuming you were a billionaire-bagger who'd gatecrashed and somehow persuaded Adam to bring you along. Unless there's something I'm missing?'

Adam had been right. Helen's reporter antennae were practically quivering under the glittering lights of the chandeliers. Alarm pumped her veins with adrenaline; it was time to gear up and play her allotted role.

'Nope, you're not missing anything,' Olivia said. 'Here I am.' Spreading her arms wide, she could only hope her tone wasn't as hollow as her tummy. 'The genuine article.'

Helen tilted her blonde head to one side, a small frown on her face. 'Well, in that case I shall watch with interest. Adam's dating technique will add a definite frisson to my article.'

Great! Just what she needed—more frissons. Heaven help her, because right now the thought of Adam's dating technique was causing her tummy to flutter with a stampede of butterflies.

There came the Adam Masterson smile again. 'Knock

yourself out, Helen. But don't forget to interview all the people who donated auction gifts and get plenty of photos of the guests.'

'Yada, yada. Don't worry. I could do this in my sleep. Consider it done, darling. Enjoy yourself, Olivia.' With a little finger-wave Helen disappeared into the crowd.

Hah! *Enjoy?* As if *that* could happen; she was already garnering avid glances laced with speculation or envy. 'What now? I think she's suspicious.'

'Maybe. But all we have to do is display a dazzling show of dating technique and all will be well.'

'Oh, super-duper. Is that meant to make me feel better?'

'It's all I've got.' He started to walk forward. 'There's no need to panic. Follow my lead, look adoringly at me and we'll be fine. All we need to do now is circulate.'

All?

That was easy for Adam to say, because he was obviously born to circulate. Olivia could only watch him in admiration as they trekked around, her heels sinking into the plush carpet, on an endless circuit of the magnificent room.

Adam made sure he spoke with each and every individual guest—a laugh here, a gesture there, serious or jokey as the occasion warranted. But he also subtly promoted the auction at every turn. No wonder he didn't bring a date to this event; his focus was on working the room as host, leaving Olivia with nothing to do except be decorative.

Which gave her way too much opportunity to watch him. To study the way his body filled out his tuxedo to perfection. To appreciate the breadth of his chest, the power of his thighs, the lithe stride. To admire the planes and angles of his face, lit and shadowed by the glittering shards of illumination.

Little surprise her hormones refused to stand down; fuelled by unfamiliar attraction, intoxicated by his nearness, by his tantalising woodsy scent, they didn't know whether they were somersaulting or cartwheeling.

The result was a strange heat in her tummy, a dizzying awareness of Adam that wouldn't go away.

His broad thigh pressed against hers during the lavish dinner, making it hard to balance her food on her fork let alone appreciate the melt-in-the-mouth four courses.

Focus, Olivia. On the beautifully decorated table with its intricately folded napkins and stunning centrepieces of cream flowers. On the sparkle of the floating candles. On anything other than Adam Masterson and the flame of desire that licked her insides every time his arm brushed hers.

Madness. This was sheer, unprecedented stupidity.

The evening took on a surrealism in which her entire being was caught up in Adam Masterson. She was mesmerised by his auctioneering power as he stood on the podium and used a mixture of charm and unquestionable sincerity to entice bids so high that Olivia felt she was on a gigantic Monopoly board.

Problem was, *she* was the Scottie dog. Practically panting over Adam Masterson. Self-disgust mingled with panic as she gulped down fizzy water in the hope of cooling herself down. This was nuts.

Wrenching her gaze away from the podium, she sighed. Adam Masterson embodied everything she disliked: rich, arrogant—he was way too reminiscent of her mum's boyfriends. To say nothing of the fact that Olivia Evans didn't pant over *any* man; she wouldn't give one the satisfaction of having that level of power over her.

'No one believes a word of all this, you know.'

Olivia looked up from her study of the snow-white tablecloth and beheld a well-known face and figure. *Oh, just freaking fabulous.* Here was a woman whose pictures Olivia had pored over in the fashion magazines—an ice-blonde supermodel who had partied with designers galore, a woman Olivia would normally have loved to speak to. But instead of discussing style this was going to be a grown-up version of the playground.

Candice's iconic lip twisted into a sneer as she slid her svelte body, clad in shimmering gold, onto a chair to the right of Olivia. 'Genuine article, my ass.'

'Excuse me?'

'You heard me.' The supermodel crossed her legs, presumably to reveal the thigh-high slit in her dress to best effect. 'You're just another cheap 'n easy bagger after Adam's money and a quick shag you can run to the tabloids with.'

The venom-tinged arrows hit their mark, but Olivia was damned if she'd show it. Gripping her hands round the edge of the table to hide their tremor, she pushed the memory of childhood taunts from her mind and met Candice's gaze. *Play it cool, Liv.*

'And you are…?' Olivia asked, sensing that the idea of not being recognised would lance the model's ego—or at least divert the attack.

A hiss showed she'd bullseyed the target, but before Candice could respond Olivia heard the chair to her left scrape back across the marbled floor.

'Candice, here, paid good money to be here tonight in the hope of bagging Adam herself.'

Olivia turned as another catwalk regular, Jessie T, vivid in an electric blue sheath dress, dropped gracefully into the seat. Olivia's stomach plummeted; this really was the resurrection of her childhood nightmare—only instead of being surrounded by pigtails she was surrounded by stylish coiffures. For a second she was tempted to push the table over and do a runner.

Until the newcomer gave her a ghost of a wink as she pressed one elegantly manicured turquoise fingernail to her cheek. 'In fact, let me see… My guess is that Candice sees herself as a "high-class" bagger, who is after one night of making sweet love before she gets herself a slot in *Frisson* or *Glossip*. Sound right, Candice?' Jessie grinned as Candice pushed her chair back and rose to her stillettoed feet. 'She's just annoyed that her plans have been foiled by you, darlin'.'

With a swing of her trademark raven bob Jessie turned her back on her rival, apparently impervious to her poison-tainted glare, until finally Candice sashayed away towards the podium.

'Hey, Olivia, I'm—'

'Jessie T. I know. And…um…thank you.'

'No worries. Adam asked me to keep an eye on you. He figured you might have to take some flak.'

Olivia blinked, feeling that insidious warmth resurging in her chest. Adam might be using her as a shield but he was doing his best to protect her, as well.

'Don't look so surprised. Adam's a good guy. Hell, darlin', if I wasn't a happily married woman I'd give you a run for your money.'

Before Olivia could come up with a response Jessie rose to her feet with feline grace.

'Have fun. But a word of warning—watch out for Candice; she can get her panties in a tight twist if things don't go her way.'

The dark-haired woman turned and high-fived Adam as he approached the table, before heading towards a group that contained her Hollywood producer husband.

Olivia looked at Adam and wished her pulse-rate would calm down. 'Thanks for asking Jessie to look out for me. And…' she nodded at the podium '…you did an amazing job up there.'

'No problem—and thank you.'

There was pride in his voice, pride and something else. Almost as if he had a personal stake in the charity. Which would explain his dedication all night, his attention to every detail, and the way he had interacted with those guests whose lives had been touched by the terrible pain of cancer.

'It's a great cause,' she said softly.

'Yes, it is.' Silence lingered in the air between them and he rubbed a hand over his face as if to clear unwelcome thoughts. 'Now it's time to dance.'

Dance? 'I'd rather not.' In fact she'd rather stick needles under her nails. Because instinct told her that until she got her errant body under control dancing with Adam was a disastrously bad idea.

'It wasn't a request.' There was that steely undertone again—the voice of someone used to getting his own way.

'And I don't take orders.' Irritation added to her jangled nerves as she glared at him. Clearly *his* hormones weren't tripping over themselves at the thought of a dance with her.

'Helen has requested photos of us dancing, so I suggest we provide them. She's not a fool. Plus, she can hardly have missed how jumpy you are.'

'Of course I'm jumpy. Posing as your date isn't easy on the nerves. Especially as I haven't been briefed. I don't know the first thing about you.'

Brown eyes crinkled in sudden amusement. 'Most of my dates don't; I wouldn't worry about it.' He held out a hand. 'Come on, Olivia. Will you dance with me? One dance. It might be fun.'

Now, that really wasn't playing fair.

He'd knocked the moral high ground from under her feet in one deft manoeuvre. As for his smile… A curl of heat spread through her midriff right down to her toes.

She tucked a tendril of hair behind her ear. 'I truly can't dance.'

'Just follow my lead.'

'I wish you'd stop saying that.'

'Come on,' he urged again. 'We need to lull Helen's suspicions.'

Unfortunately Adam was right. 'I'm not sure her watching me stumble round a dance floor will help anything,' Olivia said as she stood up. 'But, hey, what's a little public humiliation?'

'You can't be *that* bad.'

As though on his say-so she would suddenly develop balletic ability. Olivia huffed out a sigh. 'Yes, I can. I'm totally uncoordinated. Penguins dance better than me. Don't make me make an utter idiot of myself.'

'Hang on tight and you'll be fine.'

Yeah, right. Hang on tight to which bit, exactly? Hanging on tight to any part of Adam seemed a terminally bad idea.

What was the matter with her? Her body had never, ever reacted to a man like this. Sure, her relationships had entered the bedroom, but the va-va-voom hadn't really revved up until… Well, quite a long way into proceedings. If she were brutally honest her bedroom dealings had been mostly va rather than va-va, and voom had rarely been accomplished.

Whereas now they weren't even in the vicinity of a bedroom, they were *in public*, and they hadn't even kissed. Yet her body was accelerating forward, fuelled by high-octane desire, and she couldn't find the brake.

Now they were on the wretched dance floor and Adam enfolded her waist, his fingers burning through the silky thin material of her dress. The breadth of his palm imprinted on her like a brand as he pulled her closer. Heat scorched through her; he was so close…. Firm, hard muscle pressed against her. His breath tickled her newly sensitised earlobe.

'You need to relax.'

As if *that* was going to happen; a bucketload of Valium wouldn't relax her.

'Arrgle…' The noise was all she could achieve.

She could see Helen seated at a table on the edge of the dance floor, directing the photographer.

'You're doing fine,' he murmured. 'But help me out a bit more here. Maybe put your arms round my neck.'

She did as he suggested and came flush up against his wide chest. Her breath caught in her throat and she watched his brown eyes darken, his pulse throb at the base of his neck. Olivia tangled her fingers in his hair and her lungs went on strike.

Suddenly an inability to dance was no longer her prime source of concern. There were more pressing worries. Literally. Her brain issued commands at military speed. *Don't melt. Don't dribble. Don't stroke. Don't lean your head on his chest. Do not get too close.*

It was all too late. Her eyes closed. Her body moved tight up against his. Her hips circled. Searched. Needed. Found an unmistakable reaction.

Her eyes flew open as a shiver shot through his broad frame; exultation flamed that *she* had caused it.

Olivia had forgotten where she was. Who she was. What she was. All she knew was this. This was real. Bone-meltingly real.

The music came to a stop.

Mortification loomed as she remembered exactly where, who and what she was. She was plastered to him; they might as well have been having sex on the dance floor.

For a timeless moment she felt the accelerated thud of his heart against her palm, looked up into eyes that had deepened to molten copper. Then he blinked, his eyelids lifting to reveal nothing more than speculation in their brown depths.

'That should do it,' he said.

'Do what?'

'Lull any lingering doubt in Helen's mind. *And* free me from any unwanted attention from other women.'

Humiliation arrived and encased her with an icy dose of reality.

Adam had orchestrated the whole thing—staged a scene designed to convince the most sceptical of reporters. But it couldn't all have been an act. No way had he faked what had happened in his trousers. What was *still* happening in his trousers. Whilst she was *still* glued to him.

Stepping backwards, she looked up at him, wanting answers.

This was all too much. Never had she been so out of control.

'So,' he said, his voice light. 'Give me ten minutes and I'm all yours.'

Lucky her. She was out of her depth and she didn't even know how to swim. 'I don't need all of you.' *Really?*

'Then you can have whichever parts you want. How's that?'

He stepped forward and her breathing quickened in response as his woodsy scent re-assaulted her already battered senses.

'I...' She needed to time to think, to dunk her body into an ice bath and enable her brain to regain perspective.

Instead, acting of their own will, her feet propelled her towards him to bring her right up close and personal with the hard bulk of his chest and the hardness of his still very present erection. *Well, hello again.*

'Come on,' he growled, the rasp of his voice clenching her tummy muscles. 'We're leaving.'

From somewhere a small modicum of common sense asserted itself. 'But what about the guests?'

'There's a free bar and plenty of food. They'll manage.'

'But...'

'Shh.' Adam laid a finger against her lips, the rough skin tantalising the softness of her mouth.

Olivia swallowed and the final vestige of self-preservation will-o'-the-wisped away into the sparkling hum of the ballroom. Her hand reached out and slipped into his and, oblivious to the murmurs of the guests, she walked with him across the ballroom floor.

To her surprise he retained her hand in his as they half walked, half ran across the marble foyer towards the lifts. Somewhere in the recesses of her brain a voice was hollering for her attention. Screaming at her that what she was doing was downright stupid. But as she gazed down at their hands it seemed to her that, injudicious or not, it was inevitable.

From the moment she'd seen Adam a fuse had been lit; the demon of desire had sizzled and snaked its way into existence and was demanding its sinful needs be met.

The lift door swished open and he tugged her inside, barely waiting until privacy was ensured before pulling her towards him.

CHAPTER FOUR

ON SOME LEVEL Adam knew this was a bad idea. Olivia Evans was a mass of contradictions and a billionaire-bagger to boot. But he just didn't give a damn. That dance had oozed desire. Her whole being had breathed out pure raw need, promised imminent fulfilment. If he'd been capable of thought he would have sworn that all Olivia wanted was to share his bed.

And now here she was, all her professions of caring about what people thought cast to the winds.

The soft curves of her body fused against him, and her apple scent was a further intoxicant. Adam leant back against the steel wall of the lift and offered thanks to the heavens it was for his private use only. So there was no reason not to taste those lush lips right this minute, not to plunder the mouth that had taunted him the whole evening long.

Her hazel eyes met his gaze, brimming with passion. Lifting a hand, Adam swept the mass of strawberry blonde hair off her face and cupped the angle of her jaw, gently smoothing his thumb over the plump softness of her lower lip. She exhaled, a small shudder running through her.

'I've wanted to do this all evening,' he murmured. 'Touch you without anyone watching.'

'I thought it was for show.'

'It was. Didn't mean it wasn't driving me crazy.' He caressed the bare skin of her shoulder, felt the ripple of goose-bumps his fingers left in their wake. 'This is for real,' he said, dipping his head to butterfly kiss the light sheen of desire that glistened across her collarbone.

The tang of salt mingled with the sweet infusion of apple and the taste sent heat straight to his groin.

With a sigh she tilted her head and he followed the trail to the crook of her neck; her breathing quickened and he felt her body quiver in response.

'Adam?' The question was a whisper as her fingers gripped his shoulders. 'Kiss me.'

The hounds of hell couldn't have stopped him now.

The texture of her lips blew him away—soft, lush, a hint of coffee mingled with cinnamon. An exhalation of surrender escaped her as she wrapped her arms around his neck and massaged his nape, then thrust her fingers into his hair, sending shockwaves down his spine.

Her tongue touched his tentatively and primal need jolted him as he skimmed his fingers down her back and cupped the curve of her heart-shaped bottom. Olivia moaned into his mouth and rubbed against him with an urgency that rivalled his.

The lift pinged to a stop and Adam gave a growl of pure frustration before reaching out and hitting the door's close button.

Olivia didn't even seem to notice. 'Want more...' she murmured against his mouth.

Small fingers pushed at his tux jacket and, understanding her intention, he shrugged it off, the heavy material falling to the floor with a thud.

'Better?' he asked.

'Better,' she said, tugging at his shirt buttons greedily, deftly pulling the edges of Egyptian cotton apart. 'Much better.'

She gave a small grunt of pleasure as she slid her hand

underneath; her touch electrified him—set up a chain re-action headed due south.

'My turn,' he growled, and tore at the zip of her dress, glissading the silken material downward so it shimmied to the floor.

No bra. Sweet Lord. Olivia stood tall and straight and stepped over the pool of black silk. Naked except for flimsy lacy knickers and the lime-green sandals.

'Perfect,' Adam breathed. Her breasts were large, her waist slender, hips voluptuous. A body he had every intention of worshipping for hours. 'Olivia, you are so very beautiful.'

And he was so very hard that any second now the tux pants would have to give.

A small frown etched her wide brow; almost as if he'd said something wrong. He kissed the frown away and cupped the heavy weight of her breast, his thumb swirling over her erect nipple.

A guttural moan escaped her lips to rebound in the steel confines of the lift.

He couldn't wait. He needed her responsive body writhing under him, at his mercy. Desperation roiled in his gut, his hard-on painful.

Damn it.

'While I would love to take you up against that glass plate, we have no protection.' His chest pumped as he hauled in air. He wanted her so damn bad. 'I need to get you to bed, Olivia. *Now.*'

She nodded, her face flushed, eyes wide and shell-shocked as he stooped to pick up her dress, held the silken black folds for her to step into. Stopping only to grab his tux and her clutch bag, he jabbed at the lift button.

Crowded thoughts tried to surface but he pushed them away. Instead he enclosed Olivia's hand; somehow it seemed imperative to keep a connection between them.

Fumbling in his pocket for his keycard, he tugged her along the plushly carpeted corridor.

One-handed, he slid the rectangular plastic in and waited for the green light. 'Come on,' he muttered, and heard her small breathless laugh beside him.

Finally, *finally* the key mechanism clicked and he pushed the door open to reveal the immense vaulted corridor that led straight to his bedroom.

Next to him Olivia froze, and without further warning she dropped his hand in an abrupt, almost savage movement.

'Olivia?' His brain tried to compute her reaction, struggling to function when his whole body was on high alert.

Her gaze flickered rapidly, eyes wide. Crazy though it seemed, it looked as though she were conducting an in-depth survey of her surroundings.

This was the benchmark suite for all his hotels. The height of luxury—all sleek lines and on modern trend. There were flashes of abstract colour on the cream walls, gleaming wooden floors chosen by one of London's most iconic designers.

Her strawberry blonde head turned to study the lounge, the decadent enclave visible through the clear glass sliding door. Long dark eyelashes swept down once, then twice, before she slammed her hand onto her forehead.

'What the hell am I doing?'

She took another step away from him, her expression dubbing him the equivalent of Genghis Khan.

'I thought *we* were about to fulfil all our fantasies.'

Olivia winced, and for an insane moment Adam wondered if he'd imagined the past twenty minutes. Yet the tint of desire still touched her skin and his erection still ridged his pants.

'I need to leave,' she said.

'Whoa.' Adam stretched over to lean a hand against the door. 'Not so fast.'

An expression flashed across her face so akin to fear that affront seethed in his chest.

'Olivia, I'm not planning on keeping you here against your will, or taking anything you aren't offering. But after what just happened you can't just leave. Not without some sort of explanation.' His libido was desperate for some sort of elucidation, ever hopeful of a reversal in fortune.

Hell, there was a part of him tempted to pull her back into his arms, confident that her body would overrule whatever misgivings she was so suddenly exhibiting. But he couldn't do that—not after that flare of trepidation.

'So, spill,' he continued.

The tightness of her shoulders slumped fractionally but her body was still braced for fight or flight. Neither of which he would permit.

'I made a mistake,' she conceded, her voice taut, her hands smoothing the silken folds of her dress. 'It's as if I was caught in some sort of fog. A dream.' She stared at him, her chin jutting out. 'Now I've woken up.'

Disproportionate disappointment contracted his gut as the marvellous fantasies he had woven dissipated into the perfectly controlled air of the corridor.

Adam hauled in breath and willed his body to stand down—preferably every bit of it. After all, he'd weathered a lot worse disillusionment than this in his life, and it could be that Olivia was doing him a favour. Had he *really* wanted to let himself be bagged by any woman, however beautiful?

Answer: yes, he had. But if it wasn't going to happen then it wasn't going to happen. Time to move on.

He dropped his hand from the door and shrugged. 'Your call, Olivia. But for what it's worth I think we'd have been pretty awesome together.' They'd have been more than that; every instinct told him their bodies would be the perfect fit.

Her eyes skittered away from him, focused once more on the interior of his hallway. Though what was so damn fascinating about it, who knew?

'Maybe... Maybe not,' she said, placing a hand on the doorknob. 'I'll go down to Reception and get myself a room, but we need to sort out a time that we can talk. About Zeb.'

Zeb. *Damn.* He'd lost the plot, the dialogue *and* his brain. The import of her words slam-dunked and he thumped the palm of his hand right back against the door.

'Excuse me?' he said.

'Remember?' she said. 'The *baby.*'

She had to be kidding. 'The mythical baby? I thought you'd abandoned the whole "my mother is pregnant" bagging route. You can't just pick it back up now you've decided not to spend the night in my bed.'

Olivia stared at him. For a moment sheer shock rendered her speechless and her jaw threatened to hit the floor. Adam still believed she was another of those awful gold-digging women.

Worse, she almost couldn't blame him. She'd behaved exactly the way Candice had described her—cheap and easy. After a public display on the dance floor she'd kissed him in the lift, dropped her dress and allowed him a quick grope. If she hadn't been stunned back to reality by the opulence of his penthouse suite she'd have dropped her knickers, as well.

'I am not here to *bag* you.' Her words were so hopelessly inadequate she cringed. 'If I were I would have slept with you.'

'Nope.' A shake of his dark head accompanied a blaze of contempt. 'I think you've got your eye on the greater prize, Olivia. You nearly let yourself get carried away, but one look round here and you remembered just in time that there's more money to be had from a pregnancy scandal scam than a few hours in my bed.'

Oh, hell. She could see how it all made a certain hideous sense to Adam. How to explain to him that seeing this opulent bachelor pad had brought back to her the fact that Adam was a billionaire, a moneyed man who wanted her because she was beautiful—nothing more.

Just as all those rich men who'd peopled her childhood had coveted Jodie for her looks. At least her mum had put a price on her acquiescence; Olivia had been willing to give it away.

Taut silence enveloped them as Olivia gazed down at her sandals. Lime-green, with a tangerine flower carved from wood. Chosen to add pizzazz to the black dress. When it came to clothes, she knew what she was talking about. When it came to what had happened in the past hour…? Not so much.

All she knew was that she had to make this right. Because the baby was all that mattered. Guilt twanged in her chest that she had allowed her hormones to overrule that fact.

'Everything I told you about the baby is true. I realise I've screwed up. I understand you're suspicious. But please just give me half an hour. It doesn't have to be in the morning. We could do it right now.'

Adam held her gaze for a long moment, his fingers drumming on one muscled thigh. Then he gave an exasperated grunt, ran a hand over his face and back up through his hair.

'Fine. Let's *talk*.'

Pivoting, he turned and led the way into the enormous lounge, buttoning up his shirt as he walked. Relief and determination whipped around her tummy, along with a frustration she didn't even want to acknowledge. *Just great.* Her brain might have clocked the sheer awfulness of her actions but her body hadn't even begun to come to terms with the deprivation of promised pleasure.

Well, tough.

Control. She would *not* let lust control her. *Her* body, *her* hormones, *her* control. Sex was power—she *knew* that. It was a glittering token that could be used for or against you, and the only way to make sure you were on the right side was to be the one in charge.

Olivia had not been in charge in that lift; she'd been a woman possessed.

'Drink?' Adam had reached a black lacquered drinks cabinet of a type that looked as though you needed a degree in physics to open it.

'Please.'

Neither of them had touched a drop of alcohol all evening and a drink sounded a mighty fine idea. Perhaps it would knock the lust demon out so she could concentrate on conversation. Perhaps she should just swig from the bottle.

'Whisky OK?'

'Perfect.'

Like the play of his large capable hands as they deftly unstoppered the decanter.

Olivia tore her gaze away and stared around the room; better to focus on her surroundings than on the hands that had so recently touched her bare skin with such devastating effect.

'Wow!' She'd been so mesmerised that she'd actually missed the stunning effect of the floor-to-ceiling window that spanned an entire wall. Walking over, she gazed out at the lit-up panorama of London. 'The view is mind-blowing.'

'It never gets old,' he agreed as he moved next to her

and handed her a thick cut-crystal tumbler containing a generous slosh of amber liquid.

'Thank you.' With an effort she kept her voice steady despite the brush of his fingers activating that all too familiar shockwave through her.

'But I'm sure you don't want to waste your half an hour on the view,' he added. 'So take a seat and say whatever you have to say.'

With one last glance at the purple-black night sky, looking for a handy shooting star, Olivia turned away from the window and headed for the sofa.

Adam followed suit, dropping onto a cream-coloured couch.

He sprawled opposite her, crystal tumbler held loosely in one large hand, mussed dark hair glinting with copper in the muted overhead lighting. Olivia gulped down a slug of whisky in the hope that the fiery trickle would deaden his infernal impact on her senses.

She reached out for her evening bag, opened it and pulled out an envelope. Leaning forward, careful not to touch him, she handed it over and watched as he lifted the flap and pulled the photograph out.

'That's your father, isn't it?' Olivia said eventually. Not that she needed to ask: from the moment she'd seen Adam Masterson's image on the Masterson Hotels website she'd known. The likeness between the two men was too obvious for them not to be related. Enough that she hadn't even bothered researching him further. 'The woman in the picture is my mum. Jodie Evans.'

'That's Zeb,' he acknowledged. 'But this hardly proves he is the father of Jodie's baby.'

'It puts them both together at the right date, and, well, they look…' Olivia moistened her lips. 'Pretty relaxed together.'

And that was as far as she was prepared to go. She already had way too much knowledge of her mother's sex life—had spent too many nights of her childhood with her pillow over her head.

Adam didn't look as though contemplating the finer details of Jodie and Zeb's relationship was causing *him* any joy, either. His features scrunched into a scowl as his fingers drummed a tattoo on the leather arm of the sofa.

He nodded at the photo. 'When was this taken?' he asked.

'Four months ago. In Hawaii. Mum went there for a couple of weeks with friends.'

'Where she just happened to hook up with the father of a billionaire?' Disbelief dripped from his tone. 'Or did she target him in the hope of a pay-off?'

'What are you? A fully paid-up member of Cynics R Us? Mum didn't do anything of the sort. She doesn't need money.' Pride and determination pulled her spine straight. Neither Jodie nor Olivia Evans would ever rely on a man again, because now Olivia earned enough for both of them. Exactly as she had always vowed she would

'Everyone needs money, honey.'

'Not us. And you'd better believe it!' Hauling in a breath, she tried to see it from Adam's viewpoint. 'I get that you are sceptical, but this would be so much easier if you could just acknowledge I *might* be telling the truth.'

He raked a hand through his already rumpled hair and exhaled heavily into the cloud of silence. 'OK,' he said finally. 'I'll meet with your mother, see if her story checks out.'

'No!' The yelp escaped her lips too sharply and her panicked vehemence caused a hike of Adam's dark brows. 'You can't do that.'

'Because?'

Olivia clenched her hands into fists, thoroughly annoyed with herself for not anticipating his request. '*Because* Mum doesn't know I'm here.' Her conscience stabbed her with pins galore and had her squirming on the plush seat. 'If you must know she doesn't want Zeb to know about the baby.'

His face was immobile; each feature might as well have been hewn from granite. 'Why not?'

'She says it was a holiday fling and she won't burden a man with a child she knows he doesn't want.'

Adam's jaw tightened, his movements a little jerky as he picked up his glass. 'But you disagree with her?'

'I feel like a complete heel for going behind her back— but, yes, I do.'

'Why?'

The shadow in his eyes told her the question was genuine and that if she had any hope of convincing him she was going to have to answer. Not ideal. But if revealing her personal history would swing Adam's support then there was no choice.

Swallowing in an attempt to dislodge the pebble of discomfort that clogged her throat, she met his gaze. 'Because I grew up without a father and I want this baby to have a chance to have one. It's as simple as that, Adam. I promise.'

CHAPTER FIVE

ADAM DRUMMED HIS FINGERS on the arm of the sofa, the rapid tattoo making his knuckles ache.

Olivia's words had vibrated with sincerity, plucking an unwilling chord of memory within him.

Remembered frustration churned his guts. Desperate to know something about his father, his childhood self had pored over the single photograph he'd possessed. He'd plagued his mother for details until he had realised that Zeb Masterson wasn't exactly one of her favourite people. However much she'd tried to hide it.

In all conscience he couldn't doom another child to that experience.

An experience Olivia had shared.

The idea tugged at his chest, creating an unwanted connection between them. If, of course, she was telling the truth. About anything.

'What happened to your father?' he asked.

Shimmering eyelids swept down and up again as she surveyed him, her small frown indicating that she was pondering her answer or maybe even whether to answer at all.

'You brought the subject up,' he pointed out.

'I never knew him. My mother was very young when she fell pregnant—I'm lucky she kept me at all.'

She said the words with great care, as if she were stepping cautiously across the stepping stones of truth and missing out a fair few on the way.

Suspicion tingled Adam's nerves as he looked back down at the photograph. 'Jodie must have been *very* young.' The woman in the photograph couldn't be much over forty now.

'She was.'

'So it was a teenage romance that went too far?'

'Does it matter?' After a careful scrutiny of his face she huffed out a sigh and slammed her glass on the table. 'You think I'm making it up, don't you?'

'It's a possibility I'm considering, yes.'

'Fine. If you must know my father paid my mother to keep his identity secret. They struck a deal. He handed over a lump sum, she swore never to reveal who he is. Even to me.' She shifted on the sofa, clasped her hands together on her lap in a pose of defiance. 'Satisfied?'

Not really. Because he could sense her pain, knew she was telling the truth. Which moved him way into schmuck territory for forcing her confidence.

'Then *he* missed out,' he said. 'Not you. A man who would do that isn't worth knowing.'

Olivia blinked and a smile curved her lips for a fleeting second. 'Thank you. That's a way better response than saying how sorry you are.'

'You're welcome.'

The atmosphere tautened around them. His eyes snagged on her mouth and a memory of the taste of her kicked his pulse-rate up.

Her eyes shuttered again. 'It's also good to know that you *can* actually be nice. So, Mr Nice Guy…' The wedge heel of her sandal tapped on the wood of the floor. 'Will you help me?'

Adam locked on to those determined hazel eyes, half pleading, half insistent.

He tore his gaze away and rose to his feet; he had to break this spell Olivia was weaving. Instinct told him that she was telling the truth; further instinct told him that in this case his instincts were less than reliable—fuzzed and blurred by inordinate desire and a strange, tenuous bond that he would love to deny but couldn't.

Walking to the window, he stared out, forced his brain at least to make an attempt at logic. Olivia Evans could be a con artist extraordinaire. Or she could be telling the truth. In either case, logically he couldn't risk letting her go. If she were at his side she would either slip up and he would expose her web of deceit or he would remain in control of the situation.

There. Thinking was so much easier staring out at the cosmopolitan glitter of London by night. Even if the net result was dubious.

He turned to face her. 'OK,' he said. 'I'll contact Zeb.'

'Really?' A huge sigh escaped her lips as her shoulders dropped—the expelled tension was almost visible. Rising to her feet, she moved towards him, her hips swaying with an unconscious femininity. 'Thank you.'

She rested a hand on his forearm. Her touch was warm and yet it shivered his skin.

'If you could give me his phone number, I'll—'

'Not so fast. *I'll* contact him, Olivia. I'll talk with him and then we'll take things from there.'

She stepped away from him. 'No, no, no. That doesn't work for me, Adam. I want to be the one to tell him; I need to *see* his reaction. I don't know how all this is going to play out, and I don't know what your father will say or do. But I do know I need to be there when he says or does it.'

'No.' It was time to make a stand, to stop being sucked in by her beauty and do what he knew to be right. 'This is not negotiable, Olivia. Take it or leave it.'

She opened her mouth then closed it again, her protest

swallowed down even though anger flecked the hazel eyes with green. 'What happened to Mr Nice Guy?'

'This *is* Mr Nice Guy. You want to see Mr Not So Nice? Because *he* would've had you booted out of here long ago. Which is still a possibility. So, take it or leave it.'

A pause during which her eyes narrowed before, 'I'll take it. For now. But only because I'm beat. I'll head to Reception and sort out a room.'

'I've got a better idea.'

'What?'

'Stay here.'

'Say *what*?' Tiredness fled the room and Olivia wasn't sure which emotion to run with in the seething mass left in its wake. Anger vied with a certifiable urge to comply and won. Just. 'Are you *nuts*? I told you already what happened earlier was a mistake. An aberration. A…' However many more words for *mistake* there were in the thesaurus.

'Calm down.' The authoritative tone shut her up. 'The majority of my guests, including Helen Kendersen, are staying here tonight. It's included in the ticket price. Given they all believe that you're my date, it's probably better if you stay here. In the *spare room*.'

'Oh.' Now she felt like a gigantic idiot. Worse, she had the horrible idea that she sounded disappointed.

He raised his eyebrows. 'Unless, of course, you've changed your mind and you want to take up where we left off earlier?'

The words, faintly mocking, reminded her that Adam still didn't fully credit her story. Regardless of that, sleeping with Adam would mean the loss of any respect he had for her. To say nothing of the blow to her own self-respect.

'No. But thanks for the offer. And the offer of the spare room. I agree it would be more sensible if I stay here tonight.'

'That's sorted, then. Nate has had your bag sent up here anyway. Is there anything else you need?'

Your body. The answer popped into her mind, proving to her that she might as well found Idiots R Us.

'A spare toothbrush would be good.' Nothing sexual about a toothbrush. So focus on that. Bristles, plastic handle, toothpaste, flossing… Nothing attractive about that. 'If you've got one?'

'This is a hotel, Olivia. We provide multiple toothbrushes.'

Toothbrushes. He was talking about multiple toothbrushes; she was thinking about orgasms. 'There's one in the spare room already.'

'Fabulous. Super. Take me to it. The toothbrush, I mean.'

Five hours later Olivia opened bleary eyes and gave up. Sleep with Adam a mere couple of walls away wasn't possible. Not even in a bed that had literally taken her breath away. She had no idea how much a stay in a penthouse suite would cost but the decadent round bed alone would be worth it. Sumptuously comfortable and made for sin… it was no wonder her body had spent the night craving someone to sin with.

No. Not someone. *Adam.*

Olivia huffed out yet another sigh.

Coffee. She needed coffee. No—what she really needed was a hormone transplant. But she'd have to settle for coffee.

A glance in the mirror sent a shudder of sheer horror through her. Her hair had not coped well with the tossing and turning of her fevered body; if she went outside birds would be attracted to its nestlike properties. As for the bags under her eyes—they were fit for a luggage carousel.

OK. Ten minutes to make herself at least a little bit presentable. For her own sake, of course. Nothing to do with the chance that Adam might be an early riser.

Olivia pushed the door open and padded down the corridor to the kitchen. She filled the kettle up and pulled open a cupboard in the hope of finding coffee.

There had to be coffee. All hotels provided little sachets of instant granules. Surely a hotel of this ilk would have a jar of a luxury blend?

A fruitless search found some very posh tea bags that smelt woefully caffeine-free and way more like pot-pourri than tea—and then she saw it.

Whoa.

It was the mother of all coffee machines, the type that you would need ten hours' solid sleep and two degrees in *advanced* physics to use.

Next to it was a jar of coffee beans.

Might be quicker to eat a few.

Even as she contemplated the idea a knock on the main door of the suite distracted her and caused hope to surface. Maybe it was Room Service. Maybe Adam had ordered a full English breakfast and a steaming pot of coffee and maybe they were just outside the door.

Glory be!

Olivia scuttled down the corridor.

'Don't open it!'

The peremptory command reached her ears a fraction of a second too late; she'd already tugged the door towards her.

The pop of flashlights triggered a swirl of stars in front of her eyes. Unfortunately not bright enough to obscure the hideous sight of a scavenging pack of reporters on the threshold. Thank goodness she'd brushed her hair and pulled on jeans.

Various shouts permeated her eardrums.

'How does it feel to filch a man from a woman like Candice?'

'Where is the love rat?'

Then Adam was at her side, positioning himself so that his body shielded hers from view.

'No comment,' he said evenly, and with that he closed the door with a decisive bang and a succinct swear word.

Rubbing the back of his neck, he looked down at her. 'You OK?'

'No. Of course I'm not OK. I was expecting toast and scrambled eggs and sausages and coffee and I got a microphone shoved in my face. How did they even get up here?'

'That's exactly what Nathan is finding out. And heaven preserve the staff member who gave those reporters the keycode to the lift.'

A horrible thought filtered into her coffee- and sleep-deprived brain. 'They haven't found out about the baby, have they?' she whispered.

'No,' Adam said. He gestured down the hallway. 'I'll make coffee and explain.'

'Hold the explanations until the coffee kicks in.' Olivia watched Adam, reading the message sent by the grim set of his lips and the tightness of his jaw. Adam Masterson wasn't a happy man and she was pretty sure someone was going to pay the price.

'So what's this all this about?' she asked, coffee cup in hand. 'They mentioned Candice.'

'Yup. Candice has decided to score some publicity,' Adam said. 'According to her, she and I were an item and I specifically asked her to last night's event, where she thought I was going to ask her to move the relationship to a higher plane.' Adam broke off and snorted. 'This is utter drivel. Anyway instead I turned up with you, so according to Candice I'm a love rat and you're…'

'The other woman?' Horror clogged her throat and Olivia nearly choked. 'Who stole you away from Candice.'

This was the stuff of nightmares. Her friends, her clients, her mum would open the papers and she would be revealed as *the other woman*. The other woman who had slept with a man for his money.

'You've got to do something.'

'Damn right we're going to do something about it.'

Olivia frowned. 'You really care. And I'm guessing it's not my rep that you're worried about.'

'No, it's not,' he said. 'What I care about is the fact that Candice is planning to sabotage a charity event I'm co-hosting. I've sponsored the launch of a charity fashion show. Now Candice is threatening to boycott the show, along with the rest of the modelling community, and make a call for all the other women whose hearts I've broken to picket the show.'

Indignation heated her veins. 'She wouldn't really do that. Surely that's negative publicity for her?

'I assume she thinks it's worth it to paint me as London's premier love rat.' His stride increased, covering the travertine kitchen floor in a few easy lopes. 'Particularly at a charity function that means a lot to me. I will *not* let this event be disrupted.'

'Why don't you grovel to Candice?' Olivia paused, her imagination balking at the idea of Adam kowtowing to anyone. 'Apologise for the misunderstanding, explain that we're just friends. I'll back you up on that. We'll say that I'm a friend who agreed to pose as your date to protect you from the baggers. That you hadn't realised Candice was interested in you. That you are incredibly flattered and would love to go out with her. Then she'll walk the catwalk for you and everything will be fine.'

'No.' Adam stared at her as though she were mad. 'Just

no. But accept my congratulations on your excellent imagination and ability to fabricate a story.'

'At least I'm trying. Why don't *you* think of something?'

Adam came to a halt in front of the breakfast bar and Olivia gulped. Colour her shallow, but the man was flipping all her switches.

He'd pulled a shirt on over jeans but obviously not had the time to button it up, and the black edges gaped to reveal a tantalising glimpse of sculpted chest, a light smattering of hair that arrowed down over ripped abs.

'OK,' he said slowly. 'I've thought of something.'

Apprehension lifted the hairs on her arms as she waved a hand in the air. 'What?'

'It's a two-pronged plan. First I'll get Candice to back down.'

'How?'

'I'm going to offer her three dates with Noah Braithwaite.'

'*The* Noah Braithwaite?' Olivia said. 'Hollywood heartthrob?' The penny dropped. 'Also known as Noah 'Two Date' Braithwaite.'

'Yup. Noah and I are poker buddies—I'll persuade him. Candice will jump at the chance to be the woman who got a third date out of Noah Braithwaite.'

'OK. That should work,' Olivia said. 'Could you also see your way to getting her to rescind her allegations of me being a man thief?'

'That's prong two of the plan,' Adam said, and his lips curved up in a satisfied smile. 'Candice backs down, which leaves you and I still together. So, to prove that I am not a love rat who has abandoned you, *you* are coming to the fashion show as my date. You'll be icing on the cake of my respectability.'

'No way.' The response was instinctive, wrenched from her at gut level.

The previous night had been bad enough, being paraded as a possible gold-digger or at best a trophy girlfriend chosen for her looks. Olivia had looked up that article in the sleepless pre-dawn hours and knew now what she had already suspected. All Adam cared about were a woman's looks.

'Fine. I'll sweeten the pot. You play the part of my girlfriend at the fashion show and I'll take you to Zeb. *You* can tell him about the baby.'

CHAPTER SIX

ADAM KNEW HE'D made her an offer she couldn't refuse—he just wasn't sure why he'd made it. Doubtless he could have found a different way to persuade her to continue in her role.

'You mean it?' Those hazel eyes narrowed in suspicion, her thoughts presumably mirroring his.

'Yes.' And he did.

He'd tracked Zeb down in the sleepless small hours but he hadn't rung him. The image of Olivia's face had been too vivid, her voice still echoing in his ears. Her own father had rejected her very existence, denied her an understanding of her own genetic identity and roots. No wonder she had a need to see Zeb face to face to garner his reactions, good or bad, and Adam had no idea which it would be. And so he'd dropped his phone back on the bedside cabinet and left Zeb in ignorance.

'I mean it,' he said.

'This charity event is really important to you, isn't it?'

'Yes.' He hesitated. 'My mother died from myeloma.'

Her brow pinched in empathy. 'Oh, Adam. I'm so sorry.'

He clamped his lips into a grim line; it was too late to prevent the words. 'Don't worry about it. Point is I want this event to be a success. If it goes well it could become an annual event. I'll do what I need to make it work. So are you in?'

'I'm in.' Her bare foot tapped a nervous rhythm on the underfloor heated kitchen tiles. 'What next?'

'I'll sort out Candice and then we'll let the press in. Set the record straight.'

He'd expected her to demur, but instead she nodded as she glanced round and bit her lip thoughtfully. 'I'll set the scene. The secret of a good fabrication is in the detail.'

A pang of suspicion struck; was this an oblique way of telling him that *she* was lying? But now wasn't the time to wonder—best to file the doubt away for later.

'Fine. I'll call Noah.' He pulled his phone from his pocket. 'Noah? It's Adam. Remember that yacht you lost at our last game? Here's your chance to get it back. But there's a price.'

'Isn't there always?'

Adam swivelled at Olivia's muttered words but she was on her way out of the kitchen. His gaze lingered on the al-luring sway of her hips, the curve of the heart-shaped bot-tom that had fitted so snugly in his hands.

'Adam?' Noah's transatlantic drawl in his ear pulled his mind out of the gutter.

'Yeah. Listen up…'

Half an hour later Adam went in search of his partner in crime to report. A glance into the spare room yielded nothing; the room looked completely unused. Not so much as a strawberry blonde strand of hair on the pillow.

He pulled the door closed and headed for his bedroom—and stopped on the threshold with a gargled snort. Olivia lay on his king-size mattress. Correction: Olivia was rolling around on his king-size mattress. If he'd wanted his libido to get any more excited he'd have said she was writhing.

'Olivia?'

Her body stilled, and then with careful, deliberate movements she swung her legs over the side of the bed and stood up.

'I was just…' She leant over, probably in an attempt to hide the pink-tinted angles of her cheekbones, but inadvertently giving him a glorious flash of cleavage. She tugged the duvet up to leave a glimpse of the sinfully rumpled black sheets. 'The bed needs to look like we both…*used* it.'

Her breath hitched audibly as she straightened, and hazel eyes flickered away from his as she swept her arm around the room.

'What do you think?'

Wrenching his gaze away from her, and his mind out of fantasy land, he followed the arc of her hand. Olivia's bag was on the floor by the corner of the bed. Her dress was slung over the back of a chair and…and *oh, hell*. Moisture sheened his temple as he spotted the wisp of lace peeping out from under the bed.

'Hopefully this looks as though I spent the night in here.' Chewing her bottom lip, she gave a small nod. 'I'll hang my clothes up in your wardrobe, too. As an added touch. After all, if we're saying we are serious then it may be best to at least imply I've stayed here before and I'm staking a claim.'

Doubt assailed him again, battering his mind.

'What is it?' she asked.

'Are you?' he asked. 'Staking a claim? Seems to me you're pretty practised in the art of fabrication, of making a mirage of the truth.'

Her head whipped round at neck-cracking speed. 'Say *what*? I'm doing my very best to help you out here, bolster your reputation, and you're doing what? Still accusing me of scamming you?'

'I'm simply observing that you are a self-confessed expert liar and you've certainly got a whole lot further than any other woman has thus far.' Hell, he was about to announce at a press conference that she was his serious girlfriend. No one had ever got this far. Except Charlotte.

Adam blocked off the thought. His ex-wife was not a topic he wanted or needed to consider right now.

Hands slammed on those curvy hips as she shook her head in patent disbelief. 'Believe what you like, Adam. I thought I was doing a good thing here. Candice is the one whose lies are threatening to derail your charitable event, and...' She hesitated. 'She is also sullying your reputation. That's wrong. Our lie... Well, it's not harming anyone and it's repairing the damage she's done. I don't have an issue with that. Do you?'

'Not a one,' he said. 'I'm questioning your expertise. That's all.'

Back went the teeth over the plumpness of her lower lip. Adam's gut contracted in a sudden desire to take over the action. To stop talking and start feeling.

Then she shrugged. 'I've had some experience in the art of dissembling. That's all. There were times when I was growing up when life was a bit hand-to-mouth and Mum and I needed to fabricate a believable story.'

'Who for?'

'Landlords, debt collectors, teachers... Things were a bit complicated sometimes and it was important to put on a bit of a show. No harm done, and when we were flush I always paid off any debts.'

Adam felt that insidious pull at his chest again. That sense of connection, of the shared experience of a childhood made less than stable by the antics of parents. Different experiences with different outcomes—clearly Olivia and Jodie had a bond that went a whole load deeper than any link he and Zeb had. Olivia and Jodie's had been forged in love.

Her level gaze didn't falter. 'But I'm not after anything from you, Adam. Except access to Zeb.'

'OK.' He stepped forward until they were mere centimetres apart, close enough for him to clock that her chest rose and fell in definite response to his nearness. 'Got it.'

'Good,' she said, and then the silence tautened as tension wove a web around them.

It would be so easy to tumble her backwards onto the bed and turn one aspect of their shared lie to truth.

Stop. Not possible. If he accepted Olivia's story as true then he accepted Jodie to be pregnant with Zeb's baby. So it didn't matter that he'd never laid eyes on Olivia until yesterday—didn't matter they met nowhere on the family tree: the unborn baby would link them together for ever. That would be plenty complicated enough without throwing sex into the mix.

So…

Drawing from his reserves of will power, he stepped backwards. 'You've done a great job in here. I've persuaded Candice to withdraw her story and Noah has agreed to play his part. The press will be here in about half an hour.'

'Right.' Olivia blinked and then, taking his cue, she nodded. 'I need to change. So can I borrow one of your shirts? That denotes seriousness, doesn't it? Wearing someone else's clothes—it's pretty intimate. Plus I slept in my shirt last night, so that's a bit grim, and I don't think the all-black outfit is right. It's too funereal-cum-cat burglar.'

Adam shrugged. 'Fine with me.' He gestured at the wardrobe. 'Take your pick.'

She glided over to the wardrobe and slid the huge mirrored door to one side. There was a long minute as she stared inside. 'Wow! That's a lot of clothes.' She turned. 'How long are you staying here?'

He frowned. 'I keep all my stuff here.'

'So you live here? It's your home?' Her face was creased with confusion, as though the concept was incomprehensible.

'I spend most of my time on the road, in one or another of the Masterson hotels. But I spend about a week or so a month here. So I guess it's a base.'

Olivia turned to survey the bedroom as if she were soaking in the surroundings anew. 'It's very...nice,' she said.

Nice? This was the height of luxury.

Adam followed her gaze to the enormous handcrafted wooden bed, the mirrored wardrobe, the glass desk and the flat-screen television. She'd already seen the lounge, with its enormous cream leather sofas heaped with textured cushions, the glass dining table surrounded by white leather dining chairs.

'Glad you approve,' he muttered, sarcasm dripping from his tone.

A flush bloomed in her cheeks. 'I'm sorry,' she said. 'That was rude of me. This is amazing. Honestly. Really impressive.'

'But...?' He wasn't at all sure why but he wanted to know what she thought. Curiosity, maybe, at her bizarre reaction? Other women oohed and aahed. Olivia Evans was struggling to find a suitable compliment.

Elegant shoulders lifted as she waved a hand around. 'It's just not very homey, that's all.'

Give him strength. *'Homey?'*

'Lived in. Personal. I mean, did you choose anything at all in here? Or out there? Where's the clutter?'

'I approved the design.' Irritation surfaced at the defensiveness that caused him to fold his arms across his chest. 'And I don't do clutter.'

His childhood home, where he had spent the first eight years of his life with his mother, had overflowed at the seams with knick-knacks and clutter. Maria Jonson had collected souvenirs of all her life's experiences: snow globes, vases, paperweights, statues, garden gnomes. They had all ended up in their small terraced house. Maybe because his mum had had some sixth sense that her life was doomed to end way too early.

Sadness weighed heavy in his heart, along with remembered grief at leaving that home, seeing the house and all those precious possessions sold or donated to charity by Zeb.

'Possessions clutter up life,' his newly discovered father had told him. He'd placed a light hand on Adam's shoulders. *'I know it's a hard concept, but you'll work it out. You've got a new life now, Adam. A life of adventure.'*

Words that had aroused such a conflict of emotion—sadness, excitement, guilt and fear—and set him inexorably on the path to becoming the man he was today.

Rubbing a hand over his face, Adam frowned. The past wasn't relevant right now. Neither were his interior decorating preferences. Or his attitude to clutter. *'Anyway,'* he said. 'Go ahead. Pick a shirt.'

She turned her attention back to the wardrobe and tilted her head to one side.

'Interesting,' she said. 'For a man who doesn't like clutter you sure do like clothes. What do you do? Find something you like and order it in every colour? You've got three styles in there. Long sleeves, short-sleeved shirts and T-shirts. Five colours each.'

Impressive. All the clothes were in a jumbled mass, and yet she'd analysed his wardrobe at a glance. Now she was looking at him with a disconcertingly assessing slant to her hazel eyes. To his own annoyance Adam realised he was rocking on the balls of his feet. As if he was uncomfortable.

'I asked the buyer in the boutique downstairs to stock my wardrobe. He came up, took my measurements and filled the wardrobe.'

'So an interior decorator bought your furniture, a boutique owner stocks your wardrobe, and you have nothing personal. That's so...'

Adam rolled his eyes. 'Convenient?' he suggested.

She shook her head violently. '*No.* You don't get it.' She huffed out a sigh. 'I know what I'm talking about. I'm a personal shopper.'

It figured. No wonder she looked so damn good, and no wonder she had taken such care with each and every transformation. Burglar, hotel employee, ball guest, girlfriend... Olivia knew how to dress for every role.

'I run a company called Working Wardrobes.' Pride rang in her voice and illuminated the elven features. 'But the whole point is that I'm a *personal* shopper.' Her hands gesticulated animatedly as she spoke. 'I don't look at someone and think six foot three, dark hair, chocolate-brown eyes, ripped body, so I'll buy him two pairs of designer jeans and four urban sweatshirts—' She broke off as his eyebrows rose. 'For example...' she added hurriedly. 'Taking a completely random example.'

Her face creased into a fluster of dismay and he couldn't help himself: a snort of laughter erupted.

After staring at him for a perplexed second she curved her lips into a smile and then she was giggling. A full-on giggle that bubbled forth and made him laugh. A proper belly laugh. How long was it since he had laughed like that?

Too long.

Almost as though she was thinking the same thing about herself she stopped, lifted a hand to cover her lips and stared at him.

Her eyes sparkled and she looked so gorgeous all he wanted was to step forward and plunder the lushness of her lips.

Every which way he went, that was where he ended up.

Leaning forward, she snatched a shirt from its hanger. 'I'll go and transform myself,' she muttered, and scurried towards his bathroom.

CHAPTER SEVEN

OLIVIA GULPED. THE SHEER surrealism of the situation boggled her mind.

Any second now Adam was going to walk through the swish lounge, open the door and let the press into the suite—aka Adam's home, or base, or whatever he called it—and she was going to pretend to be his girlfriend. How had this happened? *How?*

Olivia felt a small familiar roll of nerves in her tummy. This *was* like her years growing up—years when she had had to play roles varying from 'beautiful young girl throwing herself on landlord's mercy' to 'beautiful girl surprising rowdy revellers with a well placed kick'. But any second now adrenaline would kick in and she'd pull this off. Just as she always had.

She could do this. She flicked a glance across at Adam. *They* could do this. Because this time they were in it together; if she went down she'd be taking him with her.

'We've got this,' Adam said, coming up behind her. The warmth and strength of his body gave her reassurance whilst it also made her strum her with desire.

Minutes later Adam ushered in Helen Kendersen and the photographer from the previous night. 'Good morning, you two. And thank you for this exclusive. *Frisson* is honoured.'

With a newfound awareness Olivia knew that Helen and the photographer had some sort of a relationship. Could see it in their body language. Helen looked…content—sleek and sated. The photographer had a smile on his face that said all was right with his world.

An unexpected tingle of envy twanged her nerves. If only she'd pulled Adam down onto the sinfully rumpled black sheets of his sumptuous bed. Earned the right to wear his shirt.

Focus, Olivia.

'Would you like to have a look round?' she offered. 'And Adam can sort out coffee for everyone.'

An hour later Olivia allowed herself a cautious exhalation of relief. Putting aside the fact that she'd had to pose on the bed with Adam, with a sappy smile on her face, the whole interview had gone amazingly well. In fact she was impressed with herself. Clearly her acting skills hadn't deserted her any more than her lock-picking ones.

'There is one more thing I'd like to request,' Adam said. 'I'd like you to ask the billionaire-baggers to back off.'

Time to chime in. 'Adam and I would really appreciate that,' she said. 'We need time together, time to explore these new feelings, and it would be so marvellous if we could do that in peace. Without tripping over gold-diggers every way we turn.'

'Wow.' Helen's blue eyes glittered as they rested first on Adam's face then switched in speculation to Olivia. 'All this… It sounds like serious stuff.'

Olivia leant forward and primed her vocal chords for girlish excitement. 'Well, it's early days yet. But, yes, I'm hoping that Adam will find me pretty addictive.'

She looked up at Adam adoringly, just in time to see his jaw tense slightly.

Given the smile on Helen's face Olivia wasn't surprised;

it was the face of someone swooping in for the kill. She braced herself as the blonde woman leaned forward.

'It's interesting timing.' A small pause, and then, 'Tell me, Adam, could your sudden new desire for a relationship have anything to do with the impending marriage of your ex?'

With teeth-clenching effort Olivia prevented her jaw from hitting her knees. *Always stay in character.* She tried to look as though the existence of an ex wasn't headline-grabbing news in itself. An ex what? Girlfriend? Wife?

A sideways glance showed that Adam looked unfazed, and a sliver of suspicion wormed its way into her psyche. Had the whole Candice and charity event thing been a ruse? This might have been his intention all along—to use their supposed relationship to get at his ex-whatever. *Fabulous.* Now she was a pawn in a classic tit-for-tat game.

Adam's shook his head. 'Nope. No connection there, Helen. Charlotte and I have been divorced for years and I wish her nothing but happiness.' He nodded at Helen's notebook. 'I have an agreement with her that I won't bring publicity to her door and I try to abide by my word. So, in the interests of *Frisson* covering the Dress to Support Myeloma event later today, I'd appreciate it if you left her out of the article.'

There was that you-don't-want-to-mess-with-me voice again, and to Olivia's annoyance it made her shiver.

She stared at Adam, frustration seething at her inability to read his expression. Not that it mattered—the bottom line was that he didn't give a stuff about branding Olivia anything he liked whilst dragging her into the public domain. But when it came to *Charlotte* it was clearly very different.

And how catty did *that* sound? Olivia stiffened. Surely she wasn't jealous of Charlotte? Because that would be ludicrous. Yet, however hard she tried to deny it, a tiny part of her soul was tinged green. Which didn't make sense. Olivia Evans did not *do* jealousy. Men were notoriously unfaithful and only a fool would put herself in a position to be hurt. So it shouldn't, *couldn't* matter to her if Adam did still care enough for his ex to be scheming to win her back.

Adam gripped the back of the cream sofa and wondered how long it would be before Olivia erupted. She'd held it together for the remainder of the interview, but he'd sensed the vibrations of her inner fury.

Now that Helen and the photographer had left she paced the lounge, each angry stride thumping down harder on the gleaming wooden floor, one irate kick sweeping aside the thickly patterned rug that impeded her progress.

Five...four...three...two...one... And she screeched to a stop in front of the sofa.

'Didn't it occur to you to mention you have an ex-wife?'

'No.' It was no more than the truth; the topic of his marriage didn't rate anywhere on his conversation list.

'Well, it should have. Because then I wouldn't have looked like a first-class idiot because my so-called partner didn't bother to mention he has an ex-wife stashed away. You should have *told* me.' She stopped, presumably because she must urgently need to replenish her lungs.

He hesitated. Beneath the bravado he could sense a thread of vulnerability. 'Look, I'm sorry if you felt stupid—it truly didn't occur to me that Helen would link our relationship and Charlotte's remarriage.'

Olivia frowned, as if assessing exactly how many of his words were true and how many were lies. The sceptical rise of her dark brow indicated her verdict. 'Really?'

'Of course, really. Neither Charlotte nor her fiancé are in the public eye. I didn't expect Helen to even know about their engagement.'

'So it's not true?'

'Is *what* not true?'

A roll of her eyes indicated her frustration, but Adam had no idea what she was getting at.

'Helen's link. Are you using me to get to Charlotte? To make her jealous?'

'No.' His reaction came straight from his gut. Using Olivia as a barrier against the flow of gold-diggers with her knowledge was one thing. Garnering her help to salvage his reputation and the charity event—he had no problem with that. But no way did he want her to feel that he had exploited her; the thought turned his insides over with distaste. 'Everything I said to Helen was true. I *am* happy for Charlotte—she has found a great guy and I wish them both a very happy future.'

And all Adam's research had indicated that Ian Mainwaring should provide Charlotte with exactly that. Ian was worth a hundred of him—would look after Charlotte, give her love, a family... Everything Adam had promised her and failed to provide.

Memory echoed in his ears: her tears, her pleading. Her voice. *'You've broken my heart, Adam. I trusted you and now you've broken my heart.'*

Aware of Olivia's direct glance, Adam commanded his expression to be neutral. 'Bottom line is I am not trying to make Charlotte jealous. That's the truth.' The words sounded too serious; her gaze caused him a thread of discomfort at the sensitive subject at hand. 'Scout's honour,' he added, turning his lips up in a smile as he glanced at his watch. 'And now that's settled we'd better get a shake on. We need to be at Somerset House at five o'clock for the show.'

As anticipated, the information deflected her from any further questions. 'Five o'clock? But I haven't got a proper dress or...'

'Just buy whatever you need. The hotel has a boutique, or if you want to hit the shops I can get someone to go with you.' For an insane moment he nearly offered himself up on the shopping altar. Almost. He didn't shop. Full stop. He had no intention of starting now.

'I'm a personal shopper. I'm quite capable of shopping by myself.'

'Nope. You'll take one of Nate's men with you.'

Hurt lanced her eyes, along with a healthy dollop of anger. 'What do you think I'm going to do? A runner?'

'No. I'm worried a reporter will make you uncomfortable, and I'm worried Candice may try and get to you. That's why I want someone with you.'

'Oh.' Her lips curved up into a wide smile. 'That told me. In that case, bring him on.'

Olivia surveyed her reflection. It didn't matter what she looked like. *It didn't.* Because she wasn't bothered by what Adam thought. She definitely did *not* want a repeat of that hot, predatory gaze that turned her insides squishy and sent heat shooting south. Definitely not.

There was some other explanation for the ripple of anticipation in her stomach. Perhaps it was horror that the purchase of the stunningly gorgeous, shimmering creation she wore had been chalked up to Adam.

But there was nothing else she could have done; she'd been standing at the till of an exclusive London boutique that she'd always wanted to visit and Jonny, aka her minder, had handed over a rectangle of plastic: the Masterson Hotels company credit card.

Outrage had clenched her rigid even as mortification had coloured her face. Olivia had tried to protest. But all her objections had fallen on deaf ears and stony ground. Jonny had been obdurate; he'd been given an order direct from Adam and as far as he was concerned it was more than his job was worth not to follow it to the letter.

So Olivia had capitulated, salving her conscience with

the determination to repay Adam at the earliest given opportunity.

An almost savage swipe of glossy pink lipstick and she was done. And she still couldn't help but imagine Adam's face when he saw her.

Stupid. Stupid. Stupid.

She'd chosen the dress for its suitability and nothing else. Her reflection stared back at her—the perfect trophy girlfriend that any respectable businessman could be proud of. The spitting image of her mother, chosen for her looks. Adam himself had admitted it, and the article had been clear. Only the beautiful should apply.

And she qualified.

The dress screamed elegance and discreetly whispered class. The simple column cut skimmed her curves and the shimmering silver fabric swooped to just touch the floor, allowing her red-painted toenails to be glimpsed in the folds. The lacy top of the dress scooped around her neck and the short sleeves showed off the toned slenderness of her arms. Her hair was held back at the neck, leaving a side fringe to fall across her forehead, and she'd opted for the fresh-faced look with her make-up.

It was perfect, and worth every one of Adam's pennies.

Yet her soul felt tainted, further polluted by the fact that she actually wanted Adam's approval—wanted those brown eyes to darken and smoulder when he looked at her.

Olivia clenched her nails into her palms. This was plain *wrong*—for a variety of reasons that all bunched together around her chest, squeezing her tight with panic.

The knock on the door set her heart pounding. She had to get a grip. Had to gain control and squash all these feelings pancake-flat.

'Coming,' she called, and walked to the door, pulling it open. Her throat dried as she drank in Adam's appearance; if he'd looked gorgeous the night before, he looked positively sinful now. The dark suit was simple and fitted perfectly around the breadth of his shoulders. White shirt and silver tie, and that woodsy scent that made her dizzy.

Adam looked as shell-shocked as she did. His arms rose as if to touch her and then dropped to his sides. A slow smile touched his lips. 'You look superb, Ms Evans. You will outshine the entire catwalk and I will be the envy of every man there.'

His words were the equivalent of an iceberg's worth of cold water, cementing what she had already known. Confirmation that Adam wanted her on display to ensure his image hadn't been too tarnished by the exploits of billionaire-baggers and supermodels. As far as he was concerned that was what his credit card had bought and that was what he was entitled to expect.

A frown slashed his brows together. 'What's wrong?'

'Nothing. I'm glad I've come up to expectations.'

'What does that mean? I've told you—you look sensational. What's the problem?'

'There is no problem and don't worry. I won't disgrace you. I know the drill.' She'd grown up watching it, after all. How to dazzle with a smile, how to make the man you were with think he was the bee's knees, wings and stripes.

'Then let's go.'

Adam held his hand out and Olivia stared at it.

'Save it for the cameras,' she said, and saw the flash of something that looked perilously like hurt cross his features. Steeling herself to ignore it, she swept past him and headed for the front door and the waiting limo.

Once inside the car Olivia slid into the furthermost corner and listened as Adam pulled out his phone. His conversations all concerned the forthcoming event and amply demonstrated just how involved Adam had been in the organisational details.

Dropping the phone onto the leather seat, he reached into his inner pocket and pulled out a sheaf of paper.

'Is that your speech?' she asked.

'Yup.' He looked down, his lips moving as he ran his eyes down the sprawling handwriting.

Olivia leant her forehead against the cool of the window and silently castigated herself as shame wormed a warm trail through her body. Adam cared about this event because it raised money for a charity that tried to combat the disease that had taken his mother from him. And she was sitting here cavilling over the fact that through no fault of his own he needed a girlfriend on his arm to demonstrate his respectability.

Yuck. She was so busy worrying about what people would think of her, so caught up in her own emotional baggage, that she'd shoved her head straight up her own backside.

The limo glided to a stop and Adam placed the papers next to him and hauled in a breath.

'Adam?'

He turned to her and her tummy dipped.

'This event is going to be great,' she said. 'You'll wow them.'

Without letting herself think she slid across the seat, her dress skimming the smoothness of the leather, until they were thigh to thigh. Twisting her upper body, she smiled at him before cupping his jaw in the chalice of her palms. She leant forward and brushed her lips against his cheek. Her heart gave a pang at the realisation he must have shaved specially. Not a trace of the stubble that had grazed her face the previous day remained.

'Your mum would be proud of you. I know it.'

Before he could react, before she could throw caution to the winds and kiss him properly, she rubbed his cheek to get rid of the light gloss of pink she'd left behind, then shimmied back along towards the limo door, which Jonny had pulled open.

Olivia stretched out her hand to Adam. 'Let's go,' she said.

They emerged from the sleek black car into the swarm of fashionistas who thronged the environs of Somerset House, home to London's Fashion Week. The crowd of assorted styles and bursts of colour had Olivia swivelling and turning, feeling ideas sparking from the incredible array of combinations and patterns.

But through it all—down the red carpet that led to the enormous domed marquee, even as she smiled the smile and walked the walk for the camera—the thought of Adam filled her mind. His ripple of nerves as he'd practised his speech had moved her, shifted something deep within her.

As they left the crisp cold of the February evening to enter the marquee Olivia caught her breath. 'It's spectacular,' she murmured.

The canvas walls were lit by the bounce and eddy of multi-coloured lights in all different shades of blue that created a magical aquamarine display reminiscent of a fairyland. Garlands looped the ceiling and the ticket-holding guests were being shown to seats that held a complimentary goody bag.

'I'd better go and make sure everything is going to plan behind the scenes,' Adam said.

Olivia nodded. 'I'll stay here. I don't want to cause Candice to have a last-minute meltdown.'

'You sure?'

'I'm sure. Truly, Adam. Please don't worry about me.' She smoothed her hands down the soft lapels of his jacket, allowed her hands to linger on the muscular wall of his chest. 'You've got this.'

'Thank you, Olivia. I appreciate it. Truly.'

For a breathless heartbeat she thought he'd kiss her. Instead he squeezed her hands before releasing her. Turning, he headed backstage.

Heart still thumping, mind whirling, Olivia headed for her seat, picked up the goody bag and looked inside. An ornate card gave her a free stay in any Masterson Hotel, inclusive of travel, complimentary spa time, meals and drinks. A mini bottle of champagne stood alongside an expensive designer body spray.

And there in the corner nestled a tissue-wrapped package with her name scrawled on it—surely in Adam's handwriting? Olivia unwrapped the light blue folds and pulled out a delicate silver charm bracelet. A surreptitious glance around showed that no one else sported anything similar on their wrist.

Surprise and appreciation lodged deep in her chest as she saw the shape of the charm dangling from the chain. It was a wardrobe: an exact copy of her company's logo. A miniature wardrobe, complete with arms and legs.

Who knew how he'd got one made so fast? She'd only told him about Working Wardrobes that morning.

She clasped the silver chain around her wrist as the lights changed to illuminate the stand at the head of the catwalk. Conversation slowly cascaded away into an expectant silence as Adam and his co-host, Fenella Jowinski, a famous model of yesteryear, emerged from the shadows into the spotlight.

Following a short, pithy speech from Fenella, Adam stepped up to the microphone and Olivia clenched her hands together as she willed him good luck vibes. Not that it would be possible for anyone to guess he was nervous, the slight whitening of his knuckles as they clasped the edge of the podium the only clue. Otherwise his body was relaxed, his voice even and melodious without a hitch or a hint of edge.

'Ladies and gentlemen, and everyone else in the audience, I'd like to thank you all for being here today to support a cause that is very dear to me.'

Here Adam paused, his eyes scanning the crowded chairs and resting for a moment on Olivia.

'I had a speech all prepared—a speech full of statistics and stories and leaps in medical advances. It was a great speech, and I spent a very long time writing it. However, thanks to some words said to me just moments before my arrival here I've changed my mind. Someone said to me that my mother would be proud of me. I hope with all my heart that that is true. So, before we get down to the business of fashion and let loose the wonderful, dedicated women who will model some amazing creations, I would like to tell you about my mother—the wonderful woman who shaped my life for eight years.'

Olivia stilled. Only eight years? That meant Adam would have been just a child when his mother died.

Pressing her lips together to hold back a gasp of empathetic pain, she leant forward, wanting to hear every word.

'Maria Jonson was truly beautiful, inside and out. She had the capability of bringing joy and light to a room with the power of her smile. A single mother who gifted me a carefree childhood, she loved life and lived every precious second of hers to the full. She didn't have a glamorous job—she worked in an accounts department—but she had an imagination that soared.'

Olivia's heart twisted with pain as Adam painted a picture of a brave, wonderful, ordinary woman. A woman who'd sung and danced and read him stories. One who'd loved movies and spending time curled up under a duvet with her son and a bowl of popcorn. A woman who had collected so many knick-knacks and souvenirs of her life that their small house had overflowed.

A woman who had suddenly contracted myeloma and three months later passed away.

'I watched her get weaker, I watched her suffer, but right to the very end she gave me love. And that is why I am standing here today—because I want this disease to be stopped. So that it no longer can claim any more wonderful, ordinary, beautiful women like Maria Jonson. My mother. A woman who deserves to be remembered. I hope wherever she is now she is proud of me, as I am still proud of her.'

You could have heard the proverbial pin drop as Adam stepped down, and Olivia marvelled at what he had done. He had brought his mother's memory to life and he'd done so without being maudlin or displaying an ounce of self-pity.

Compassion and grief cloaked her at the thought of an eight-year-old Adam whose whole life had been wrenched topsy-turvy, desolated by the loss of the person who had meant everything to him. And for it to have happened so fast... He must have been terrified, alone, hurt and angry at fate.

Questions swirled around her mind—where had Zeb been? Not once in his speech had Adam even mentioned his father.

'Well, hell. I never knew *any* of that.'

Olivia jumped at the deep American drawl coming at her from her left. The large, craggy-featured blond man who must have seated himself whilst she had been deep in reverie gave her a warm smile, his dark blue eyes creasing.

There was no mistaking who it was: Noah Braithwaite—star of a string of box office hits. Amazing that she hadn't even noticed his arrival—the man was all about charisma—but her focus, her entire body and mind, had been tuned to Adam.

'You must be Olivia.'

'Yes.' Olivia forced herself to smile and shoved her feet firmly down on the smooth canvas floor of the marquee.

Racing across the catwalk towards Adam was not an option, however hard her body ached to hold him. He wouldn't thank her for it. The last thing he needed was for her to make some sort of public display when he had refrained from anything of the sort.

'I'm Noah. The man your enterprising boyfriend has sacrificed to Candice.'

'You got your yacht back,' Olivia pointed out a touch tartly.

'True. But never fear. Adam'll skin me of it again next poker night.' As if seeing her bristle, Noah grinned. 'Relax, Olivia. I'm teasing you. Adam knows damn well I'd have done it for nothing but the sake of friendship. I'm just hoping Candice isn't as big a diva as she's made out to be.' He winked. 'Speaking of whom, I'd better go to my allocated seat, where I can best see my three-date woman, or she'll throw a hissy fit.'

Olivia watched the show in a daze as models shimmied, sashayed and glided down the catwalk. Silks and satins and tweeds all interweaved in a dazzling display of talent and outrageous ingenuity. But even as she exclaimed in appreciation of the outlandish and the exquisite her gaze kept flickering back to Adam, pulled by a magnetic need to make sure he was all right.

It was a yearning that she had to hold in check until the end of the show when finally, *finally*, she wended her way through the crowd towards him.

CHAPTER EIGHT

'THANK GOODNESS THAT'S OVER.' Adam slid into the glossy limousine after Olivia and expelled a huge sigh. Unaccustomed weariness rolled over him and he flexed his shoulders before leaning back against the padded leather and tugging his tie off.

Two hours of mingling, of accepting condolences and congratulations, and he felt raw. Exposed, even. He'd managed to field the more personal questions, had tried to speak simply of his mother and the woman he remembered her to have been. Or maybe didn't remember enough.

'Do you regret your speech?'

He turned to look at Olivia, her profile silhouetted in the muted light of the car, shadows playing on her beautiful features.

Unease threaded him as he realised how good it had felt to have her by his side. His disquiet was almost enhanced by his feeling of gratitude when he remembered how she had shielded him where she could, her touch on his arm a balm.

And here he was, waxing lyrical.

The emotional impact of the whole event had quite simply temporarily knocked his perspective off course.

'No,' he said. 'I don't regret it because I do want her to be remembered.'

'It can't have been easy,' Olivia said, her voice low, warming him. 'But you did well, Adam. Really well. Maria *would* have been proud of you. She sounds like an amazing woman and an amazing mum.' She hesitated, twirling a stray tendril of hair round her finger. 'It must have been devastating for you when you lost her.'

He could shut her off, could simply say that he didn't want to talk about it. But to his own surprise he didn't mind. Olivia had stood by him all evening and helped him deflect exactly the same comments from strangers.

'I *was* devastated, and I had no idea how to deal with it. You could say I handled it badly.'

She shifted across the seat, turned so her upper body faced his, the silver of her dress shimmering in the dusky light. 'I think that's understandable,' she said.

'I was angry,' he said. So angry he could still feel the heat of it scorch him across the years. He'd been helpless and scared and he'd hated it. 'Angry with fate, with life. I was even angry with her for dying. For not somehow fighting it. Guess I took it personally.'

'I don't think there's any other way of taking it,' Olivia said.

He glanced at her. 'Is that how you took your dad's behaviour?'

'Yes.' Elegant shoulders hitched. 'My head tells me that he would have rejected any child. But my heart and soul knows he rejected *me*. Difference is my father had a choice. Your mother didn't.'

Adam nodded. 'I know that. I guess I feel bad that back then I was more caught up with what was going to happen to me than caring about everything she'd lost.' A guilt that had been enhanced further by Zeb's arrival. It had taken his mother's death to bring him what he'd wished for so fervently. The knowledge still soured his gut.

Next to him, Olivia shook her head. 'Don't even think about beating yourself up.'

A slender hand touched his arm, a tendril of hair wisped over his cheek and her smell enveloped him.

Close—she was so close—and, damn it, he didn't want to talk any more.

Or think any more.

He just wanted to feel.

Her hazel eyes met his, their green flecks glowing in the dimness of the car's interior as she scanned his expression.

There was no hesitation. In one lithe movement she moved closer to him. Elegant fingers reached up and cupped his jaw. Her fingers were so slight and gentle and yet they branded him. Her touch glided over his stubble and around to the nape of his neck; the caress jolted desire through his system.

He released the clip that held her hair back and dug his fingers in the glorious silken tresses, angled her face towards him.

Olivia parted her lips and his name escaped into the air—part groan, part entreaty. Shifting closer to her, he lowered his lips to hers. Her scent swirled round him and he was lost. Caught in a spirally vortex of desire. He could taste the fizz of champagne that lingered on her lips, and when his tongue stroked hers she moaned softly into his mouth, her fingers curling into his shirt.

Closer… He needed her closer. Adam spanned her slender waist with his hands and hoisted her onto his lap, cursing at the constraint caused by the long silver folds of her dress.

With a murmur of frustration Olivia hitched the shimmering material up around her waist and straddled him, her long, smooth thighs pressing against his. Adam's now almost painful erection strained at his zipper, pushing against her hot core.

Fingers splayed, he smoothed up the soft bare skin of her thighs and she shivered in response. Her breathing quickened as he tiptoed his fingers farther up and reached the wispy lace of her knickers.

She was so wet, so responsive. His hips jerked upward and she writhed against him; their movements bordered on being frantic.

Breaking the kiss, she straightened. Magnificent. More beautiful than anything he'd ever seen before. Hair tumbled in wild disarray around her flushed face. Hazel eyes dark with a primal desire.

'Adam, please...' she murmured, her voice ragged.

He slid his finger under the lacy edge of her knickers, desperate to watch her shatter for him.

'I'm right here.'

And her expression changed. The glow of desire receded and her face leeched of all colour as she stared down at him with a look of sheer horror.

In one awkward movement she twisted from his lap and desperate, jerky hands pulled the shimmering folds of her dress down her thighs.

She leant back against the seat and lifted her hands to her face. A muffled curse escaped her fingers.

Adam forced his breathing to a regular pattern and tried to calm both his veering heart and his hard-on.

'Olivia—' he began.

She shook her head. 'Please don't say anything. I'm sorry. And I'm mortified. And I really want to somehow pretend this didn't happen.'

'Again?' He couldn't help himself; frustration and confusion roiled inside him. 'No can do, Olivia. It happened. *Again*.'

'I'm sorry, Adam. I'm behaving like an idiot.' She dropped her hands from her face and shifted even farther away from him. 'Clearly my body is having some sort of

hormonal meltdown. But I will not give in to it. I *hate* this.
This attraction. I just want to turn it off.'

Despite himself, he smiled. 'Attraction doesn't work
like that. You can't just turn it off.'

'I can. I have to.' Her voice vibrated with desperate
conviction. 'Attraction is nothing more than a chemical
reaction.'

'Exactly. And you can't change chemical reactions.'

'No, but you can make sure that you don't drop the po-
tassium into the water.'

'Or you can enjoy the explosion,' he said.

'And pick up the pieces later? Not my style.'

It wasn't his, either. The important thing for him in
any relationship was mutual short-term enjoyment, after
which both parties went their separate ways in—and this
was key—one piece. He'd created enough mess to last him
a lifetime. A memory of Charlotte's tearstained face ac-
costed him and it was all the reminder he needed.

So what the hell was he doing now? Enjoyment did *not*
include sharing his feelings about his mother's death. Talking about Maria to keep her memory alive was one thing;
spilling his guts to Olivia was a whole different situation.

And, whilst he had no doubt there would have been
plenty of instant and mutual gratification going on if she
hadn't pulled back, that wasn't the point. Shock rendered
him mute. He hadn't so much as considered any of his
usual rules and regulations—hadn't even bothered to find
out Olivia's views on relationships.

Way to go, Adam.

So an explosion was a sucky idea, however hard his
hard-on was. Olivia Evans had issues. She was emotional
dynamite and it was time to get out of the laboratory. There
would be other women, other attractions. *But not like this.*
No, not like this—and a damn good thing, too.

'Not my style, either.'

'Then we're agreed,' she stated. She plunged her hands into the shimmering folds of her dress as she turned to face him. 'So let's move on. I've done my part of the deal. Now it's your turn. You need to take me to Zeb.'

'Ah. Yes. That.'

'Yes. That.' Her eyes narrowed in sudden suspicion. 'Don't you *dare* renege on our deal.'

'I'm not. It's just a little bit more complicated than I mentioned.'

'Complicated how?'

'Zeb's in Thailand.'

There was a pause as Olivia's lips, still swollen from his kisses, opened and closed.

'*Thailand?* He's thousands of miles away and you didn't think to mention it?'

Adam felt her outrage and welcomed it; at least it dissipated the sexual tension that still whispered in the air. Plus, anger was as good an outlet for frustration as any, and he knew that Olivia must be feeling plenty frustrated. She'd pulled herself from the brink of orgasm. Come to that, he wasn't feeling any too relaxed himself.

Served him right for being so quick off the mark and for letting this whole situation get out of control.

'I didn't see the need,' he said. 'I'll honour my side of the deal. I'll take you to Thailand.'

'Just like that?'

'Sure. It's a few hours away by plane. We pack. We go.'

'I can't just up sticks and fly to Thailand. When's Zeb coming back?'

Ah. 'He's not.'

'What do you mean? He *lives* in Thailand?'

'Zeb doesn't live anywhere.'

Olivia frowned. 'So he's like you? Does he live in a hotel?'

The innocent question scraped Adam's nerves; if only

Olivia knew how like his father he was. 'Zeb's a modern-day nomad.'

Dismay etched Olivia's beautiful features; her hazel eyes drenched with disbelief. 'But he must have a…a base? Somewhere? Give me something here, Adam.'

'He doesn't have anything,' Adam said flatly. 'No address at all. Zeb believes that bricks and mortar are an unnecessary responsibility. He very rarely stays in the same place for more than a few weeks and he goes wherever the whim carries him.'

'But where does she leave his things? His possessions?'

'He carries them with him.'

'You're kidding me?' She bit her lip. 'It's not exactly what I was hoping for.'

No doubt she'd been hoping for the full package: a man who would be happy to have a child, would settle down and play happy families complete with white picket fence.

He pushed down the surge of sympathy; it was better for Olivia to know it as it was. 'Zeb is a wanderer. He won't change that for anyone.' He rubbed a hand over his face. 'It's a Masterson trait, Olivia,' he said, trying to keep the bitterness from his voice. 'We don't do settling down.'

Zeb hadn't, and Adam certainly hadn't. He'd tried—hell, he'd tried. He'd married Charlotte with high hopes of that white picket fence for himself. Hopes he'd dashed to the earth a mere two years into the soulless purgatory that settling down had turned out to be. For him. Not for Charlotte. Charlotte had been in her element, nest-building, whilst the chintz-patterned wallpaper had been closing in on Adam.

'It's not possible. But that isn't the point. Nomad or not, he still needs to be told about the baby. So we'd better get ourselves to Thailand.' Sort this fiasco out, then life could return to normal.

'It's not that easy.'

'Sure it is. Leave it to me,' Adam said as the limo glided to a stop outside the imposing front of his Mayfair hotel.

The deep throb of the aeroplane's engines reverberated in Olivia's ears. Just twenty-four hours later and she was on her way to Thailand. Ko Lanta, to be precise. Excitement surfaced as she looked down at her tablet, where a glorious picture of a white sandy beach evoked relaxation. According to the blurb, the island was a veritable paradise—a scenic miasma of forest, hill, and coral-rimmed beaches.

Unfortunately Olivia wasn't going to Ko Lanta to admire the verdant beauty of the island or to absorb the sun's brilliant rays. Her remit was to meet with Zeb. Yet the anticipation refused to recede completely, still fizzed defiantly in her tummy. Worst of all, she had the feeling that the reason for its existence wasn't the hotness of her destination—it was more to do with the hotness of her travelling companion.

She eyed Adam across the aisle of the private jet and felt heat seep into her skin; embarrassment still fresh over the whole crazy hot-and-heavy interlude in his limo. The only saving grace was that she'd stopped it. On the verge of what had promised to be the mother of all orgasms.

Yay. Nice timing, Liv.

Served her right. Shame twisted her tummy at the memory of herself straddling him in the back of a car, Adam's hand up her skirt, the plea in her voice as she'd begged him for release.

Double yay!

This whole overwhelming attraction was so confusing. All she'd wanted to offer Adam was solace—not a quickie in the back of his car. Mind you, looking at him now, she had no idea how she had dared even to offer him comfort, let alone anything else. The past few hours Adam had been utterly unapproachable, a veritable machine of efficiency while she'd run around sorting out cover for her work for a week. But the man who had confided in her, the man who had kissed her senseless and nearly robbed her of every last vestige of control had vanished.

Which was a *good* thing.

The sigh she emitted was way too loud; Adam looked up from his laptop.

'Is there something you need?'

'Nope. I'm fine.'

'Good.'

His attention was diverted straight back to the screen and a thoroughly irrational annoyance sparked inside her. If he'd deigned to tell her more about Zeb a little bit earlier instead of clinging to his stupid belief that she was a billionaire-bagger, maybe she might have had more time to prepare for this trip. Plus, how come he got to sit there all cool and collected whilst she sat here reliving the scene in the limo?

She sighed again, even louder, and tapped her nails against the table in a deliberate beat.

'Olivia. If there is a problem please feel free to share. What is it?'

'I was just wondering why you insisted I take a week off.' An outright fib, but she didn't care. It might be childish but she wanted him distract him.

'Because it makes sense. Zeb comes and goes as he pleases. He only got to Ko Lanta a couple of days ago, so he should still be there. But if he's moved on we'll need to track him. It's not worth the risk of losing him again.'

Her sigh was genuine this time; Zeb wasn't exactly turning out to be the kind of man she had envisaged when she'd embarked on this search.

Though, come to think of it, Adam still hadn't told her much about Zeb at all, really. A sideways glance confirmed that he had returned his attention to his laptop and clearly figured their conversation to be closed. His expression was shuttered, his forehead creased in a frown of concentration.

Olivia hauled in breath. Well, tough. They would be in Thailand soon, and she'd be meeting Zeb shortly after. Surely she was entitled to some information about the man?

'Adam?' she said.

'Yes?'

Impatience tinged the air as he looked up and Olivia stiffened her spine.

'Could you tell me something more about Zeb?'

'More?' Dark eyebrows rose, for all the world as if he'd already given her a three-tome biography of Zeb. 'There isn't any more to tell.'

'Sure there is. So far all I've got is a man who wanders the world and has no wish to settle down.'

'What else do you need to know?'

Olivia shrugged. 'Well, what sort of father was he?' She hesitated. 'I noticed you didn't mention him in your speech, and...' And, man, she was an idiot. The penny plummeted down. 'That's why your mother brought you up on your own. Zeb didn't stick around.'

Adam's lips set in a grim line before he let out a whoosh of air and leant back, pushing his laptop back. 'No, he didn't,' he said.

Compassion, confusion and anger threaded through her. 'And you didn't think to mention this earlier?'

'No, I didn't.'

Keep calm, Liv. 'Care to expand on your reasoning?'

'Sure. Zeb walked away when my mum told him she was pregnant. Thirty years ago. Doesn't mean he'd do the same now. Plus, when Mum found out how ill she was she hired a PI to track him down. Zeb turned up a few weeks after the funeral and took me with him on his travels.'

His tone was way too bland. Olivia knew right down to her tippy-toes that there was a lot more to the story. The set of his lips also informed her that that was all she was going to get.

'And? What sort of dad was he then?'

Adam shrugged. 'He was exciting, unpredictable, fun. He taught me how to play poker and how to look out for myself.'

A shadow crossed his eyes on those last words, and Olivia would swear the air had become tinted with a wisp of bitterness.

As if he realised it Adam tipped his hands in the air and smiled. 'He made me into the man I am today. I'm pretty happy with that.' The plane started its descent and Adam snapped his laptop shut. 'And on that note, it looks like we're here.'

Olivia gazed out the window and for a minute wished that she was here on a holiday, visiting a country she had only dreamed of.

A sigh of sheer appreciation escaped her lips as they disembarked into the incredible warmth of the Thai sun. She shrugged off her light cardigan and tipped her face up to the sun's rays. Deep warmth suffused her as the sun soaked into her skin.

'Incredible,' she murmured as she followed Adam across the tarmac to a waiting taxi. 'So, two hours and we'll be on Ko Lanta?' she asked.

'Less. I've got a taxi booked, and then a speedboat. I've got seasickness tablets if you need them.'

'I should be fine. I haven't been on many boats, but I've never thrown up, either.'

'It's a bit bumpy, and you may get a bit wet, but it's the quickest way to get there.'

The remainder of their trip was achieved in silence, and anticipation built in Olivia with each bump of the car over the long, dusty road. Hope looped the loop in her tummy as she inhaled the salty sea spray and the speedboat skimmed the glittering turquoise waves. The journey was bringing them inexorably closer and closer to Zeb.

A man walked towards them as they stepped off the deck of the speedboat onto the pier at Ko Lanta.

'Adam. It is good to see you.'

'Gan. Good to see you, too.' Adam turned to Olivia. 'Olivia, this is Gan. He taught me how to snorkel many, many moons ago.'

The small, compact man's wrinkled face creased further as he smiled. 'Welcome to Ko Lanta, Olivia.'

'Thank you, Gan.'

'Can you take us straight to Zeb?' Adam asked.

The smile dropped from the elderly man's lips and he shook his head. 'Sorry, Adam. Your father is no longer here.'

Leaden disappointment weighted Olivia's tummy, but Gan went on hurriedly.

'He will be back. He has gone on a trip. In five maybe six days he said he will be back. But he has taken a boat and I have no way of contacting him. I am sorry, Adam. I could not stop him.'

'That's OK, Gan. It's not your fault. And it could be a lot worse. At least we know he's coming back. All we have to do is stay put until he gets here.'

All? Olivia bit her lip and tried to suppress the rising swell of panic. More waiting. More time with Adam. On a gloriously beautiful sun-drenched island where there would be no handy distractions. No reporters or charity events or work. Just Olivia and Adam, stranded on an isle.

Adam looked down at her and a rueful smile tugged his lips, as though his mind was travelling the same path as hers. 'Right now,' he said, 'I could do with a drink.'

'I'm with you on that.' Drowning her sorrows seemed like an excellent short-term solution. Maybe she and Adam could work out a way to follow Zeb, contact Zeb…*something*.

Gan nodded at their bags, then at the Jeep parked on the side of the road. 'Where are you staying, Adam? I can take your bags to the hotel and drop you off if you like?'

'Gan. You're the man,' Adam said, with a smile of genuine affection on his face.

Clearly there was a bond between the two men, which meant Ko Lanta must be a place Adam visited frequently. A pang struck her. Maybe this was his holiday destination of choice. How many other women had he brought here?

Not that the answer mattered to Olivia. In the slightest.

Fifteen minutes later she jumped out of the Jeep, waved to Gan and followed Adam to a bamboo shack beach bar. Wooden benches and tables dotted the golden sand that shimmered in the rays of evening sunshine. The beat of reggae music blended with the lapping of the waves to create an atmosphere so laid-back she could feel her frayed nerves being soothed.

Adam indicated a table and she slid along the sun-warmed teak with a sigh as a bare-chested waiter with a small drum strapped around his waist sauntered across the sand, placed a tray with two frosted glasses of beer on the table and high-fived Adam.

'Adam. Gan said you'd be here.'

'Saru. How are you doing? Where's your dad?'

The young man beamed. 'He's semi-retired now. He's away. On a cruise, would you believe? How long you here for?'

'A week or so.' Adam gestured to Olivia. 'This is Olivia.'

Saru shook her hand with a wide smile and then moseyed along to greet an arriving family, his hands beating a jaunty tune as he walked.

'Saru's a mean drummer,' Adam said. 'He and I used to busk in the old town together.'

An image of a bare-chested Adam with a drum around his muscular waist, busking on the dusky streets, sun glinting in his hair, filled her mind. So real, so vivid she felt she could reach out and touch him.

'You can play reggae? You busked?'

Adam grinned. 'I'm hot stuff.'

Didn't she know it? Olivia picked up her glass, welcoming the cold against her heated flesh. She drank, the strong taste puckering her lips even as the temperature refreshed her.

'It's beautiful here,' she said as she absorbed the sight of the sea, watched the mesh of different blues blend into an endless aquamarine expanse. 'I can see why you come here so often.' And, heaven help her, in this moment she wished she was here as one of his women.

'It's a great place to relax,' Adam continued. 'So relax, Olivia.'

'I *am* relaxed.'

A smile tugged his lips and her tummy back-flipped as her toes crunched into the warm sand.

'No, you aren't. Your leg is jigging up and down, your hand is clenched around your glass way too hard, and you have a perma-frown creasing your forehead.'

Well, no way was she about to explain that her lack of relaxation was to do with her escalating panic as to how she could spend a week in his company without losing her already tenuous grip on control.

She glared at him. 'OK. So I'm not relaxed. I was psyched up to meet Zeb and now he's not here—won't be here for days.'

Adam stretched his long legs out. 'Exactly.'

Desire and irritation jangled her nerves at his sheer carefree attitude and she took another gulp of beer. 'Exactly what?'

'There is nothing we can do except wait, so why not make the best of it? When's the last time you had a holiday?'

Olivia opened her mouth and closed it again. Surely she must have had a holiday at some point? There'd been that weekend away with her best friend, Suzi, but she didn't think that was what Adam meant. Even that had been a year ago.

She shrugged. 'Time goes so fast,' she said finally. 'And I suppose I don't want to waste money. I've got a mortgage and bills, and my mum's—' Olivia broke off.

'And your mum's what?'

Why shouldn't she tell him? It was nothing to be ashamed of. 'Allowance. I give my mum an allowance. She went through a lot to support me as a child—now it's my turn to look after her.'

Adam raised his eyebrows. 'So your mum holidays in Hawaii and you stay at home?'

'I'm happy with it that way.'

For a moment she thought he'd say more but then he shook his head. 'The point is you can't remember the last time you had a holiday. So here you are. In Thailand. Perfect weather. No work. So let go. Relax. Have a holiday.'

'A holiday?' she echoed. 'I'm here to find Zeb. Not loll about on a beach.'

'But Zeb isn't here and there's nothing you can do about it.'

'There must be something. Can't we radio him?'

'Gan tried that. No response.'

Broad shoulders hitched, his blue T stretched over the breadth of his chest and Olivia gulped.

'Accept it, Olivia. I know it's tough, but we're stuck on this beautiful island.'

'Yes, well, that's the problem, isn't it?' Olivia tried to gulp the words down but it was too late; she'd been so busy gawping at his display of muscle she'd spoken without thought.

'What is?'

'The "we" bit of it. You. Me. I'm sure that if I was stuck on this island by myself relaxation wouldn't be an issue. But you…you make me edgy.'

'No need. We're both agreed that we aren't going to act on our attraction, so surely we can get past it and enjoy some chill-out time? Have some fun? You can do that, right?'

The look he cast her was so full of challenge tempered by a glint of mischief that she was torn between the desire to slap him or sample him.

'Of course I can,' she said through clenched teeth.

'I don't believe you. I reckon you've forgotten how to wind down, Olivia. If you ever knew.'

'That is ridiculous. I am an expert at taking it easy.' She took another defiant gulp of beer. The taste was welcome, smooth, and cold as it slipped down her throat.

Adam followed suit and her hungry eyes watched, mesmerised by the sturdy column of his throat. *Enough.* They were supposed to be past the attraction—and, hell, if Adam could get past it so could she.

'I've *bulldozed* past that ridiculous attraction thing.' She waved her hand in the air. 'And I'm the Queen of Chill.'

His smile widened into what could definitely be classed as a positive grin. A wolfish grin. 'Good. That's sorted, then.' He lifted his glass. 'To our holiday.'

'I'll drink to that,' she said, and drained the glass.

Caution tried to rear its head and was instantly decapitated by the Queen of Chill. True, her head was spinning a little. True, she'd had no sleep and little food. But both those things could be remedied. Soon. After maybe one more drink.

As if reading her mind, Adam rose. 'I'll get you a refill. And some water and some food.'

'Fabulous.'

Picking up their empty glasses, he strode towards the

bamboo enclosure. He was so tall, so broad, so damn imposing and oh, so very delicious. His every stride was adding to her head-spin. Hell, by the end of a week with Mr Hotter Than the Core of the Universe she'd be eligible for a starring role in a horror movie.

Nope. Nope. Nope.

Get with it, Liv.

The attraction had been annihilated and they were on holiday. Chillaxing.

May all the gods help her!

CHAPTER NINE

AFTER CONFERRING WITH Saru on the question of food Adam exited the dim interior of the bar and paused in the doorway to absorb the dusky beauty of the evening sky.

His thoughts raced. A holiday with Olivia, brought about by Zeb's all too predictable runner. Adam had asked Gan not to mention Adam's arrival, but even so Zeb would have suspected something was up. After all it was Zeb who had taught Adam his poker table skills; he had uncanny instincts and an ability to read body language the way other people read magazines. A spooked Zeb would have seen an impromptu sailing trip as the perfect solution—would hope that by the time he came back the trouble he'd scented would be long gone.

Well, he was in for a surprise, because Adam was going nowhere.

Instead he and Olivia were going to stay here and have a holiday.

He must be nuts. *Stellar idea, Adam. Give the man a medal. For sheer foolishness.* But Olivia was in evident need of a break and the words had somehow fallen from his lips without permission from his brain. *Enjoy some chill-out time. Have some fun. Past the attraction.* Amazing he hadn't been struck by lightning for such an enormous fib.

But the point was this attraction *was* under control. *His* control, not his libido's. At the end of the day Olivia was a beautiful woman, but one who was off-limits. He was a grown-up, and he was perfectly capable of spending a relaxed few days with Olivia.

Adam glanced out to the sea, where the sun was just beginning to dip down. The sky was an electric, vivid orange speckled with tinted tangerine clouds. It was the perfect way to start any holiday.

He flicked his gaze to her, wanting to see her reaction.

'For Pete's sake,' he muttered, and strode across the sand.

Olivia looked up from the napkin on which she was industriously scribbling notes from the illuminated tablet on the tabletop.

'Tha—' she began as he placed the tray down.

Adam walked around and placed his hands on her already sun-kissed shoulders. The warmth of her skin tingled his palms as he gently turned her upper body to face the horizon.

'Oh...' She sucked in a breath of sheer wonder and his whole body stood to attention; the sound that fell from her lips held the same resonance as yesterday in the limo. For a second the sunset dimmed—a mere backdrop to the memory of her astride him, flushed and needy.

Olivia gave a small wriggle of her shoulders and he kneaded his fingers into the tight knots of her shoulders. Relaxed? This woman had a long way to go before she was anywhere near. And *he* didn't have far to go until the silken texture of her skin, her small huff of pleasure as he dug deeper, pushed him to the brink of discomfort.

Come on, Adam. Past the attraction, remember? Yeah, well, he was only human. Perhaps a friendly massage wasn't the best way forward.

Releasing her shoulders, he stepped backwards and

walked round to his seat, the distance between them a welcome one. He gestured to her list. 'So what's that?'

'It's a list of things to do this week,' she said. 'I was researching Ko Lanta.'

'I thought the Queen of Chill would be more into lazing around on the beach soaking up some rays.' Preferably in a skimpy bikini; even better if Olivia was in need of a handy sun-cream applier. Sure, his libido might not be in control, but it deserved something; he might not be able to bed her, but there was nothing wrong with a bit of healthy appreciation.

A resolute shake of her head indicated disagreement. 'I may never get to visit Thailand again—I've got to make sure I see everything.' She picked up her glass and took a gulp, then transferred her attention to the serviette. 'There's this tour where you trek through the jungle, climb up a dried-up waterfall and get to a limestone cave. It sounds awesome.'

'I know the one,' he said. 'One of my favourite places.'

'Perfect. We'll definitely go there, then. And there's a national park with a lighthouse, and loads of other stuff. First thing tomorrow I'll need to get some proper shoes and suitable clothes, though. I didn't really pack for a holiday.'

'What *did* you pack for?'

'Meeting Zeb.'

'I'm not entirely sure I'm with you.' Presumably beach clothes were beach clothes.

'Well, take this for example.' Olivia waved a hand at her outfit. 'I put a lot of thought into it. Grey trousers and a light grey tunic top. Muted colours, but not funereal. Non-threatening, non-judgemental. I was aiming for soothing and neutral.'

'Is that how you think all the time?'

'What do you mean?'

Adam glanced down. 'I look at my clothes and I think

blue T-shirt and beige chinos. You use your clothes to play a part.'

'No, I don't.'

'Then what's *your* style? Enquiring minds want to know.' His theory was that Olivia used clothes to define her, wore them as armour.

'It's all my style. I'd never wear anything I didn't like.'

'I get that. But it seems like all your clothes have a purpose—to set you up in a certain role. You're always projecting an image.'

For a second a look of confusion entered her hazel eyes. As if he'd flummoxed or at the very least flustered her.

She took another hefty swig from her glass, almost draining it. 'That's all so much psychobabble,' she declared as she put her glass down with exaggerated care. 'Anyway, you're a fine one to talk with your co-ordinated-by-some-one-else wardrobe.' She rested her elbows on the table so she could prop her chin in her hands and surveyed him a touch owlishly. 'I think you should let me dress you.' Tilting her head to one side, she gave a slightly fuzzy smile. 'Oops. That may have come out wrong.'

'Nah. It would have come out wrong if you'd asked if you could *undress* me.'

The giggle she gave was infectious, 'Seriously, though, let's go shopping. It could be fun.'

Fun? What the hell...? But maybe it would be—and it was her holiday, after all. Perhaps he could persuade her into buying that skimpy bikini or a tiny little pair of shorts that would barely cover her heart-shaped derrière. Hell, yes.

'OK. I'm in. You choose me some clothes and I'll choose you some clothes. I don't want to spend a week with you dressed in your "soothe Zeb" outfits. I want to be seen with—'

'Oh, here we go!' Olivia shook her head and her lush lips actually curled.

'Here we go, where?'

'To the part where you want to display me on your arm as some sort of trophy.'

'Olivia. What the hell are you talking about?' He poured her a glass of water and pushed it across the table.

She eyed it belligerently before picking it up. 'It doesn't matter.' She waved the glass and water droplets fell onto the tabletop. 'Let's have another drink. My round.'

'Uh-uh.' Adam shook his head. 'No more beer until you explain.'

Olivia chewed her bottom lip for a moment and then shrugged. 'You drive a hard bargain, Masterson. Fine. You want to know? I'll tell you. It's *complicated*, being beautiful.'

'Are you for real? Women would kill to look like you and you're complaining?'

She shook her head. 'It means men only want you for your looks.'

'Not only. There's more to it than that.'

'Hornswoggle.' Olivia looked impressed with the word, her lips formulating the syllables again. 'Take us, for example. You and me. Not that there is a you and me any more. But when there was. You with me?'

'Faint but pursuing. Keep going.'

'Well, *you*—' she pointed at him '—were attracted to me because of my looks. If I didn't have this face, if I'd arrived in your hotel with greasy hair dressed in a bin bag, I wouldn't have had any effect on you at all.'

'Not true.'

'Totally true.' She waved a finger at him. 'I looked up that billionaire-bagging article, Adam. Your only criteria is beauty. *"Blonde or dark. Small or tall... This field is open to all. Adam Masterson's only criteria is beauty: the man likes his ladies easy on the eye."* Not a mention of personality. So—*ha*! I rest my case and I'll go get us a beer.'

'Not so fast.' Adam snorted. 'You're quoting a rubbishy magazine article. It's hardly gospel.'

Olivia wrinkled her nose before pouring herself another glass of water. 'OK, Mr Holier Than Thou. List the last five women you slept with. Then tell me—were they beautiful or were they not?'

Adam could feel metaphorical ropes digging into his back; a sudden urge to loosen his collar overcame him and he wasn't even wearing a shirt. Those five women ranged back over a three-year period but, yes, they were all beautiful. Mind you, until this moment, with Olivia's accusatory eyes boring it into him, he'd never seen it as a problem.

'I *like* beautiful women,' he said. 'Does it count in my favour that they were all a different type of beautiful?'

'Nope, it doesn't,' she said. 'All it shows is that you like variety.' She nodded sagely. 'And what were all those women wearing when you met them? How did they look? Were they dressed to attract? Made up to show themselves at their best?'

How he wished he could claim that at least one of those five women had been met at a farm, in wellington boots, up to her knees in pig muck. But honesty, along with the knowledge that those hazel eyes would see straight through him, compelled him to admit, 'Yes.'

'Double *ha*!' Another shrug and a small smirk tugged those lush lips. 'There you have it. I win. Just admit it, Adam. Looks matter and clothes matter. Especially to men like *you*.' She jabbed her finger at his chest.

He raised his eyebrows. 'Men like me? What does that mean?' And why did he know he wouldn't like the answer?

'Men with the money to buy whatever and whomever they choose.'

'Ouch. Are you suggesting I *buy* my women?' Good thing his ego was fairly robust.

'Not exactly,' she admitted as she tilted her head to one side and studied him, a small critical frown creasing her forehead. 'You're good-looking, you're charming—*maybe* your women would date you regardless of your wallet.'

'Well, gee. Thanks for the vote of confidence.'

'My point is that your money eases your path. It means that even when you're old and wrinkly beautiful women will always be available to you and you know that. So you'll keep sampling the variety and so it will go on—for ever and ever, amen.' She tipped her hands up. 'A bit like a conveyor belt.'

A conveyor belt? 'That implies each woman is the same,' he countered. 'Every woman I date is different and I've liked every single one.' Well, he hadn't *dis*liked any of them, at any rate, and that counted for something, right? 'And—' he allowed a reminiscent smile to play about his lips, wanting her to remember he had a lot more to offer a woman than the contents of his wallet '—I'm pretty sure they all have very fond memories of me.'

Her face tinted pink, as if she were reliving the memory of their recent activities in lift and limo. But then she rallied and pressed her lips together in a line of disapproval. 'Hmmph. No doubt they do. And I'm sure you give them an expensive souvenir of their time spent gracing your bed.'

'Sure I give them presents.' Actually, he didn't even do that. He just sent them off to shop in the boutiques in whichever Masterson Hotel they were in and rack their purchases up to his account. 'And, yes, it is a token of appreciation—but there's nothing wrong with that.'

If a woman had given him the pleasure of her company and her body then it seemed reasonable to give her something back. Something that didn't cost him anything but money. After all he had more of that than he knew what to do with.

One thing he could thank his marriage for: in his lunatic attempt to prove he could settle down and reclaim the home of his childhood, he'd fallen into a career that he loved. And he'd made sure that Charlotte benefited; the alimony he paid was more than generous.

Heaven knew she deserved every red cent, because her pain had taught him the truth about himself: he couldn't do love, he couldn't do settling down. But that didn't mean he needed to condemn himself to celibacy. And if that meant a conveyor belt of beautiful women in his life, hell, he didn't have a problem with that. Not one.

'Olivia. I plead guilty to liking a moving line of beautiful women, but it's not for the kudos of having a trophy woman on my arm. I date women whose company I find enjoyable in the bedroom and out. And I make damn sure no one gets hurt.'

'How do you do that?'

'I have rules.'

She gave a small sigh. 'Of *course* you have rules. I can't believe I'm asking this, but please share.'

'Short-term, no expectations, no deep emotions, a good time had by all. That way everyone knows to jump off the conveyor belt when the ride is over. And no one gets hurt.' He hitched his shoulders. 'Works for me.'

'Not for me,' she said. 'In fact I'd rather poke myself in the eye than lose all my self-respect by even putting my toe on your conveyor belt. I refuse to be some interchangeable good-time girl, only valued for my looks and my understanding that all that's in it for me is just sex, expensive dinners and some goodbye jewellery.'

'Well, *I* refuse to be branded some rich Lothario who pays for his pleasures. And, for the record, I offer *hot* sex—not just sex.'

* * *

Hot sex.

The words lingered on the warm evening breeze along-side her own. Olivia's brain whirred a frantic calculation. Hot sex, expensive dinners and jewellery. And this was bad because...?

OK, she'd forego the latter two, but suddenly every molecule of her was asking what exactly was wrong with having hot sex with...say, Adam? In return for...hot sex with Adam.

Mutual pleasure.

So where exactly was the catch?

Oh, yeah, it was short-term. No love on offer.

She didn't want long-term. Definitely didn't want love.

So what exactly would she lose?

'Olivia?'

Her head snapped up from her unseeing contemplation of the table.

'You OK?' he asked, amusement lacing the deep voice. 'You look like you're having an internal debate on the meaning of life. And losing.'

'I am fine. Absolutely fine.'

And she was. Hot sex with Adam would mean loss of control and she would *not* go there. She'd want him more than he wanted her. She was interchangeable with any beautiful woman. The power would be all his. Bang would go her self-respect. Problem was, right now self-respect seemed highly overrated.

'Why don't we move inside?' she suggested. 'I'm sure you want to catch up with Saru and...'

'You looking for a chaperone, Olivia?'

She looked up at him, desperate to deny it, but seeing the glint of mischief and sympathy in his brown eyes she couldn't. 'Something like that.' Rallying, she managed a smile. 'I wouldn't want that bulldozed attraction to return.'

'Hell, honey, neither would I. I couldn't agree with you more. There's safety in numbers, so let's get ourselves inside.'

Rising to her feet, she picked up her empty glass and set off towards the bar, sandals crunching into the moon-dappled sand. She went up the rickety wooden steps that led to the interior of the bar and stopped on the threshold, air whooshing from her lungs.

'Wow!' The inside of the bar was a vibrant Mecca for reggae. Posters covered every millimetre of the walls, and the ceiling was looped with garlands of flags in bright red, yellow and green. Olivia absorbed the life-size cardboard Bob Marley in front of a small stage tucked into the corner. Tables half filled with customers were scattered over the wooden floor and there was a buzz of conversation against the beat of reggae music being emitted from the sophisticated sound system.

'Saru is a bit of a reggae fanatic,' Adam said. 'You should hear him and his cousin perform. They are amazing.'

'Hey, Adam,' Saru called from behind the bar. 'You want to play?'

Adam hesitated.

'Go on,' Olivia said, the urge to see this hitherto unseen side to Adam nigh on overwhelming. This was a different type of relaxed from his usual practised, laid-back charm and she wanted to witness it. 'Demonstrate your hot stuff.'

Just far away from me. Please. On the drums. Not on me. Please.

'You sure you don't mind?'

'Cross my heart.'

'Yes. Come on, Adam. Show Olivia what you can do,' Saru encouraged as he walked around the bar counter. 'Olivia, Adam has never brought a woman here before. We should mark the occasion. Sit here. I'll get you a beer.'

He tapped a man on the shoulder. 'And Marley, as he is known for obvious reasons, will sing.'

A totally stupid warmth melted over her as Adam ushered her to a table. He had never brought a woman here before. True, he hadn't exactly chosen to bring her, either, but that wasn't the point. She wasn't 100 per cent sure what the point actually was, but right now she didn't care.

Olivia watched as Adam strode to the stage and seated himself behind a pair of bongo drums. He stroked the top and drummed his fingers in a gentle experimental tattoo. Saru leapt up next to him and they had a quick whispered confab with Marley before the strains of one of the world's best-known reggae songs strummed from his guitar, the drums in perfect accompaniment as Marley started to sing.

He had a magnificent voice, but Olivia's eyes were riveted to Adam and a whole different level of desire swathed her. Utterly relaxed, lost in the moment and the music, he looked in his element. His large hands moved as if he and the instrument were one—as if he'd been born playing the bongos. When he and Saru chimed in for the chorus, Olivia picked out Adam's deep melodious voice and a shiver trembled over her spine.

Envy touched her. The idea of losing herself in something, really believing there was nothing to worry about, was alluring in the extreme. Maybe for a couple of hours tonight, though, she could do that. Be Olivia on holiday— actually be the Queen of Chill for real.

She drank another glug of beer and allowed her sandal-clad toes to tap the wooden floor. Like the rest of the clientele she found her body swaying as the set progressed. Her heart beat faster and faster as she watched Adam, his hands a blur now, his muscular forearms sheened with sweat, thick thighs pressed against the drums. He was so damn hot her insides twisted with the sheer wanting of him.

Marley bowed at the close of the song even as the clientele called for more.

Saru stood up. 'Anyone else want a go?'

A Thai man at an adjoining table jumped to his feet. 'I'll sing,' he said.

Saru plucked a guitar down from the selection hanging behind the stage. 'Elvis takes the stage,' he announced as he passed the instrument over. 'Olivia? You want to try the drums?'

It took Olivia a second to understand the question. 'Me?' she said. 'Um…I'm fine watching…but thanks all the same. I'm not really very musical.'

Then Adam looked up from the drums and made a *come hither* movement with his hand, and of their own volition her feet propelled her upward and onward. *Nooooooo!* This was the world's very worst idea. The last drum she'd played she'd been aged two and it had been saucepan-shaped. Yet she kept right on going to where Adam waited at the edge of the stage, his hand outstretched.

As his fingers clasped hers Olivia bit back a gasp even as she cursed her own imagination. Because that was all it could be. Electric currents could *not* be generated by desire; it was a scientific impossibility.

Once on stage Olivia looked around the bar, lit up by a scattering of red-, yellow-, and green-coloured paper lanterns, its relaxed patrons all chatting as 'Elvis' limbered up on the guitar. Saru drummed an impromptu solo, the haunting beat carrying on the night breeze wafting in through the open windows.

'I'm really not sure about this,' Olivia said.

'It'll be fun,' Adam said. 'Give it a go. Come on. The Queen of Chill would.'

'Ha ha!' Olivia hesitated for a moment and then pinned her shoulders back. What the hell? If she stepped off this stage now she'd regret it. After all, when would she ever get the chance to do something like this again?

It would be an experience, and it was worth the headiness provoked by Adam's proximity. He was buzzing; she could feel the vibe jumping off him. His scent assaulted her senses, the pure masculine tang of salt and his underlying woodsy scent sending her dizzy with longing.

'OK,' she said. 'I'll give it a go.'

She followed him to the bongos, dropped down onto the low stool behind them, and pulled the drums forward between her thighs. The leather was warm from Adam's body heat and Olivia shuddered.

And then she melted as he slid onto the stool behind her, the rock-solid wall of his chest against her back. A strange noise emerged from her mouth, half mewl, half groan, as his arms slipped round her waist and his big hands covered hers.

'Meep.'

'You need to sit on the edge of the seat,' he said softly, his breath tickling her ear. 'And position your legs at a ninety-degree angle.'

'Meep.'

Get a grip. He is positioning you to play the drums. Nothing else. This is not the time to channel Roadrunner.

'You OK?' Adam's voice held amusement and sin; the combination was lethal.

'Yup. Fine.'

'Good. You need the larger drum just below your right knee and nudge the smaller one to your left.'

If she focused really hard on the drums instead of the press of his body, she could do this.

'You comfy?'

'Just peachy.' Never mind that her muscles were in clench mode and it was nothing to do with drum-holding.

'Good. That's important. Make sure you've got the drum firmly in place between your legs.'

His voice was so low, so full of innuendo that Olivia was torn between a desire to elbow him or call him on it. She went for option two.

Wriggling her bottom backwards she grinned at the evidence of exactly what innuendo was doing to him. 'You sure you're talking about the drum?' she whispered.

His breath hitched and the solid muscle of his thigh convulsed against her leg. 'Excellent question. What would you *like* me to be talking about, Olivia?'

He pressed the edge of his erection against the small of her back and she moaned. She had to ground herself; she really did. They had agreed to bypass the attraction, so what exactly was Adam doing? Maybe he was being carried away by the music—in which case it was up to her to be the sane one.

'The drums,' she said hoarsely. 'That's what we're talking about here.'

'Anything you say, cupcake.' He caressed her hands, his thumbs stroking her index fingers until she couldn't think straight. 'In which case now you need to limber up,' he growled. 'You'll need to use your fingers and thumbs to do a lot of the work.'

'Meep. Meep.'

'This is what you'll need to get a beat going.' His nose brushed her cheek; he was so very close they were practically melded. Her entire body was on alert as his scent enveloped her.

Reality, Liv. Try to focus.

Saru had started playing now, and the singer strummed the first chord of the song.

'Just go with it, Olivia,' Adam murmured. 'Go with the rhythm. Lose yourself in it.'

For a second her body tensed against his and then something shifted inside her chest—a leaden block, pushed aside by the volcano of desire that was building up inside her like a fever. She closed her eyes and allowed her body to sway to the beat, encased by the strength of Adam's arms. She felt his body move with hers and dizziness soared. Her hands, still underneath his, moved instinctively to the rhythmic beat of the music until the singer sang a final harmonic refrain, the echo of his voice soaring into the warm glow of the bar.

Applause rang out and Olivia opened her eyes, suddenly aware of the insane grin on her face.

'That was amazing,' she breathed. And so was this: Adam's hard body pressed up against her, the high of having done something so out of character. She wondered if it was possible that aliens had abducted the real Olivia Evans.

'There's nothing like it,' Adam agreed.

Saru jumped down off the stage and after a long moment Adam released her waist and rose to his feet. Olivia gave a small shiver. Of cold, she reassured herself. Not loss, because that would be absurd.

Her heart still pounded, her head still spun, and desire still smouldered, desperate to erupt. Damn it, she wanted that physical connection to remain.

Without letting herself question it further she rose and twisted round, closed the gap between them in a single small step. She looped her arms round the solid column of his waist, curled her fingers into the waistband of his shorts and rocked right up against him.

CHAPTER TEN

ADAM STARED DOWN into her wide hazel eyes, saw her lush pink lips part. There was no way in heaven or hell he could resist her. One taste, one kiss—that was all he'd allow himself. After the glorious frustration of having her lush body so close, her apple scent intoxicating him whilst her sheer abandon in the music had stopped him short, a kiss was surely not too much to take?

'Adam? Please. This time I won't pull back.'

Whoa...

A kiss was one thing; Olivia was asking for more. *Huzzah.*

Somehow he had to think past the temptation to throw her over his shoulder, race back to the hotel, and take her at her word. Before she changed her mind.

'Damn it.' The words emerged from his throat hoarse and guttural. Twice they'd been carried away, and two times Olivia had hauled herself back. There must be reasons for that.

Complicated reasons.

So if she was surrendering herself now that was a huge deal for her.

Which further muddied the already swamp-like water.

About the only thing Adam was sure of now, apart from his body's urgent desire, was that complications were bad news.

For all concerned.

NINA MILNE 121

Olivia was vulnerable and that put her off-limits.

Digging deep into his reserves of willpower, he gently reached back to unclasp her grip and stepped backwards.

'No can do, Olivia.'

Her tongue peeped out as she moistened her lips. 'Why not?' A downward lingering glance and then her hazel eyes flicked back up to meet his. 'I can see that you're feeling this, too.'

'You'll get no argument there.' The thought that this hard-on now had nowhere to go was enough to make him weep. 'But we agreed. No explosion means no pieces to pick up. So help me, right now all I want to do is take you to my bed. But it's not a good idea. For either of us.'

No way was he taking that emotional journey with her. A fling with Olivia would necessarily involve more than hot sex, expensive dinners and a piece of jewellery. And he didn't want more because he had nothing more to give.

Olivia bit her lip, and his resolve faltered at the hurt that shadowed her eyes.

Then she blinked and pulled her hands from his grasp. 'Well, this is embarrassing,' she said finally, with a brittle attempt at a laugh.

'No. No embarrassment allowed,' he said firmly. 'Because there is nothing to feel awkward about. I promise. Now, come on. We deserve a beer, and after our excellent drumming performance there will be plenty of people who want to buy us one. Come on, Olivia. Let's party.'

She hesitated for a moment and then gave her small characteristic nod.

They descended the double steps leading off the stage and returned to their table where two beers already awaited them, the frosted glasses a welcome diversion from their conversation. Perhaps the ice-cold drink would cool him down. His body sizzled with disappointment at being short-changed. Whilst his libido was calling him every sort of fool.

'Cheers,' he said, raising his glass. 'To your first public performance.'

She clinked her glass against his. 'And likely to be my last.'

'Why?'

'I can't see me taking up drumming once I get back home.' There was an almost wistful note to her voice before she frowned and took another sip of beer. 'I'll buy a CD, though. That song—what sort of music was it? It didn't sound like reggae.'

'Calypso music,' Adam said. 'It's Afro-Carribean and the songs tend to represent the voice of the people. In the past the lyrics have been used politically and historically.'

This was ridiculous; the conversation was so stilted he might as well find some wooden sticks to prop it up.

It was a relief to see Saru arrive with two more beers in hand. 'Here you go. On the house, for a spectacular performance, Olivia.'

'Thank you, Saru. I enjoyed every minute.'

'Enjoy. I'll be back soon with some food for you both. Beef *phaenang*. You'll love it.'

Once he'd gone, silence loomed and Adam strained his brain to find any topic of conversation, drummed his fingers on the tabletop in time to the jiggle of her foot on the wooden planks of the floor.

She drained one beer and pulled the fresh one towards her. 'I've got an idea,' she said. 'To solve our conversational vacuum.'

'Go right ahead.'

'Let's play twenty questions.'

Good grief. Had it really come to this? The type of games he usually indulged in with his dates were more the kind you played in the bedroom. *Ah, but Olivia isn't your date. And you vetoed the bedroom. Idiot that you are.*

'Twenty questions it is.'

'Good. I'll go first.' Olivia wrinkled her nose in thought. 'What's your favourite colour?'

'Umm…' *Come on, Adam.* It was an easy question and the answer didn't even have to be true. 'Blue.'

'That's it?'

'Yup.'

'What type of blue? Navy? Royal? Turquoise? Aquamarine? Azure?'

'OK, OK. I get it. And that counted as an extra question. Navy blue.'

Olivia shook her head. 'Dull, Masterson. That's plain *dull.*'

Adam tried and failed to remember the last time a woman had dismissed him as being dull.

'Your turn,' she said.

'Where do you live?' Hard to believe that he didn't know, but he didn't.

'Bath. I love it. I moved there a few years ago and it's such a great city. It's steeped in history and it's got amazing shops, as well.'

'Where did you live before?'

'Oh, here and there. We moved around a lot. That's why I was so desperate to settle down properly. I think it's why I love my flat so much. It's not big, but it doubles as a work and home space and it's mine.' Animation lit her features, her skin taking on a luminosity that had nothing to do with the coloured lanterns. 'Do you want to see some photos?' she offered.

Guessing that it might well be Olivia's attempt to ground herself, to remind herself of home and work and the real world, Adam nodded. 'Love to.' Could be *his* resolve could do with a bit of focus, too.

Without preamble she stood up and moved her chair around so she was sitting adjacent to him instead of opposite, and he braced himself for what he was beginning to think of as The Olivia Effect.

'So, these are the "before" pictures,' she said, placing her tablet on the table between them. 'When I bought it the place needed a *whole* lot of work.'

She wasn't kidding. The pictures showed dilapidated, damp-ridden rooms. Floorboards pushed through the rotten wool of threadbare carpets, dingy wallpaper peeled off the walls.

'Now look at this. This is the work area.'

Adam let out a whistle as he saw how she had transformed the bay-fronted room. Originally meant as a lounge, it was now a professional office space. The walls were a bright, clean white, embellished with pictures of stylish fashions through the years and fabulous prints of Bath throughout the ages. Comfortable and homely overstuffed armchairs and a brightly upholstered sofa surrounded a table complete with fashion magazines. The wooden floor gleamed and the bright and cheerful rugs that littered the floor screamed *fun* along with good taste.

She beamed at him. 'And this is the kitchen.'

It was a fraction of the size of his but it looked way more personal. The blown-up photos showed a neatly put up shelf of eclectic cookbooks that covered the globe in cuisine, a row of brightly coloured mugs, and pottery jars labelled 'Tea', 'Coffee', and 'Sugar'.

'I'll bet your fridge is properly compartmentalised.'

'I'll let you into a secret.'

She leant forward confidentially, so close that he could see the light smattering of freckles on the end of her nose.

'I keep my spices in alphabetical order.'

'Whereas I don't own any spices at all.'

Which pretty much summed it up.

A stray strand of her strawberry hair tickled his cheek and lured his fingers as she shook her head.

'That's just wrong,' she declared slightly fuzzily as she picked up her glass.

'Hey! Not owning spices is hardly a crime.'

'It is from now. The Queen of Chill decrees it.'

Another shake of her head and Adam placed his hands on the table, out of temptation's way.

'Seriously, Adam, it's not right to live in a hotel room.'

'Penthouse suite,' he interpolated.

She waved a hand. 'Whatever. Point is, you never have to do anything *real*.'

'Such as?'

'Cooking. Cleaning. Dusting.'

Adam tipped his hands in the air. 'And this is a problem because…?'

'But that's what us normal everyday types have to do. I think it would be good for you to get down on your knees and scrub a bathroom floor.'

He couldn't resist. 'But I can think of so many more pleasurable activities to do on my knees. Can't you?'

Her face was tinged pink and her mouth smacked into a circle of surprised outrage, and Adam felt his lips quirk upwards into a smile.

'I can't believe you said that,' she said, before emitting a sudden snort of laughter and staring into her glass. 'Hey. It's empty. How did that happen?'

'I think you drank it.' Adam glanced up. 'Ah. Here comes our food.'

'And more beer,' Olivia said on a slight hiccup. 'Good man, Saru.' She beamed up at Saru as he placed two steaming plates in front of them. 'This looks incredible.'

Saru grinned. 'Thank you, Olivia. The ingredients are all fresh. I bought them myself from the market today.'

Leaning over the plate, Olivia inhaled. 'It smells as

good as it looks. What's in it? And do you mind if I take notes?' She indicated the napkin by her side.

Adam blinked; there was a certain fascination in watching the animation on her face as she listed all the ingredients, the tip of her tongue protruding at the corner of her mouth.

'Kaffir lime, coconut milk, palm sugar...'

Yet another first. Adam tried and failed to imagine any woman he'd dated taking recipe notes from a waiter.

'What?' she asked after Saru had left. 'I can't have sauce on my nose because I haven't started eating yet.'

'Nothing,' Adam said, shaking his head and pushing away the urge to tell her she was adorable. 'Just tuck in.'

'Don't mind if I do.'

Adam had never witnessed anyone demolish a plateful of food with such ladylike dedication. Within minutes her plate was wiped clean.

'That was amazing,' Olivia said, as she pulled her glass towards her. 'Now, where were we with twenty questions? Why don't you tell me your hobbies?'

To Adam's surprise, the next time he glanced around the bar had emptied, the music had been turned off, and he and Olivia had swapped a mountain of information. Favourite films—hers: *Breakfast at Tiffany's*; his: *The Great Escape*. Favourite book—hers: too many to count, so *Lord of the Rings* and all of Austen; his: *Lord of the Rings* and anything detective.

'I think it's time to go before Saru kicks us out,' Adam said.

Olivia nodded and then winced, placed her hands on the table and levered herself up. 'I may be ever so slightly... tipsy,' she announced. 'Not inebee...inebril...in...drunk, you understand. Just tiddly. Like in winks. That's what we should play next. Tiddlywinks.'

'Next time,' Adam said.

'Itsh a deal.' Olivia looked down and then dropped back onto the chair. 'We can't go.'

'Why not?'

'Cos I haven't got my…you know…my thingy. The thing that I wrote thingies down on.'

'The napkin?'

'Yup.' Olivia folded her arms on the table. 'Can't go without that. It's like a souvenir…you know?'

'I'll see what I can do.'

'You're a prince.'

Fifteen minutes later a diligent search had located the scrawled upon napkin and Olivia had very carefully folded it up and tucked it into her tablet case.

'Let's go,' she said, and wended her way towards the door.

There was nothing for it—no choice but to snake his arm around the slender span of her waist in order to steer her straight across the moonlit sand. His body reacted all too predictably as she tucked herself next to him, leant against him with a small, satisfied sigh.

'There we go. Easy does it, Olivia.'

'Call me Liv.'

'I'd be honoured.'

She looked up at the sky. 'So beautiful,' she said. 'All black and glittery and…and starry. Like your eyes.'

'Thank you.' Adam suppressed a grin; Olivia…no, *Liv* was going to regret this the next day.

'Adam?'

'Yes.'

'Can I ask you another question?'

'Question twenty-one? Sure.'

'What do you think about love?'

Ah. Talk about sliding in the knock-out punch right at the end. Glancing down at her, he acquitted her of intentionally wanting to catch him out. Her nose was simply crinkled in thought as she waited for his answer.

'I believe in it for other people but I know it's not for me.' He hitched his shoulders as she tilted her head, the movement casing a friction against his chest.

'Well, I don't like love. Because…'

She stumbled slightly and he tightened his grasp around her waist, his gut clenching with renewed desire.

'Because,' she continued, 'love is an illusion.'

If only the stirring of his body was a delusion. *Focus on the conversation, Adam.* Although it didn't really matter what they said because it was unlikely that Olivia would remember.

'Why do you say that?'

Olivia slid to a stop and turned to face him, held onto his arms as she peered up at his face. 'Cos it's true. Men cheat, dazzled by a beautiful face or the thrill of the forbidden, and they hop out of the marriage bed—' she snapped her fingers as she gave a little jump, scuffing up grains of moonlit sand '—just like that. Or they say they love you to get into your knickers. It's an illusion to romanticise sex.'

'Not all men are like that. Think of all the happily married people in the world.'

'Nah.' Her wave dismissed half the population. 'Another mirage. Most of them have compromised. For a lifestyle or a child. They'd all betray each other given the right price.' She heaved a great sigh. 'It's verrrry sad.'

'Would you compromise?'

'Never.' She slammed her shoulders back. 'Never give up. Never surrender. That's me. I'm not the compromising sort. And I know the truth. Remember the truth, Adam. Love is an illusion.'

'I'll remember, Liv. Now, let's get going. We're nearly at the hotel.'

Minutes later Adam surveyed the bedroom and gusted

out a sigh. Gan must have assumed they were sharing a room—more to the point that they were sharing a bed.

'I'll go and sort out another room.'

'No. Itsh OK. Really. We're past the attraction, remember? It's all over and done with.'

Clearly Olivia was suffering from selective memory and/or delusion.

She surveyed the bed. 'But just in case we'll build a barricade.'

With great precision she leant over the mattress and Adam's heart skipped a beat at the sight of her heart-shaped bottom.

Very carefully Olivia arranged an armful of pillows in a straight line down the middle of the bed. 'Easy-peasy, lemon-squeezy. Sleep well, Adam'

Somehow that seemed unlikely.

But it would be another first. Sharing a bed with a woman and a barricade; he must be losing his touch.

Olivia squeaked her eyelids open and hurriedly closed them again. Sunlight. That was definitely a clue. So was the whirr of air-conditioning.

Enough to tell her that she wasn't tucked up nice and safe and warm in her bedroom at home in the middle of a Bath winter.

Then there was the flower-sweet scent borne in on the sunlit breeze.

She was in Thailand.

Memories surfaced. Of a bar on the beach. Golden sand crunching underneath her toes. A fantastically beautiful sunset. Drums… A napkin scribbled with notes… And beer…lots of beer.

And there had been Adam.

'Rise and shine, Liv.'

'That's a joke, right? And who said you could call me Liv?'

'You did.' His deep tone was tinged with amusement. 'So, rise and shine, Liv.'

Olivia hauled her eyes open again and turned her head, wincing. 'Rising is a faint possibility. Shining, not so much.'

'I've brought tea,' he said, and stepped forward to place a steaming mug on the bedside table.

Bedside.

The word was ominous, opening the floodgates to the next wave of memory.

Olivia braced her hands on the mattress and hoisted herself up gingerly, wriggled backwards and leant against the padded headboard. She reached for the life-saving cup of tea, devoutly hoping that everything could be cured by a nice cuppa.

'Thank you,' she murmured, her tongue thick and fuzzy, but soothed by the strong brew, and her parched throat grateful as the reviving liquid slipped down her throat. 'So…' Gripping the folds of the blanket, she forced herself to meet his gaze. 'Hit me. How embarrassed should I be?'

'How embarrassed do you want to be?'

She very rarely got even so much as tipsy, and even then only if she was with someone like Suzi, whom she trusted implicitly. Alcohol was a known inhibition-destroyer and a sure-fire route to loss of control. So what had she been thinking last night? Somewhere along the line she had quite clearly dropped the ball.

Please let that be the only ball-associated activity that had gone on. What a crying waste it would be if she'd slept with Adam and didn't remember it. No. That wasn't possible. Every molecule of her would retain every second of the experience. This she knew.

'Just tell me, Adam. What did I do?'

'Nothing so terrible. Honest. I *like* sleeping with a barricade down the middle of the bed.'

His eyes glittered, and the glints of amusement were oddly reassuring. Adam was teasing her, and he wouldn't do that if she'd done anything spectacularly daft. Like climbing over the barricade and jumping his bones.

Trepidation returned and Olivia licked suddenly dry lips, heat shooting through her as his eyes followed the movement, snagged on her mouth 'Did it work?'

'Yes, it worked.' His face was suddenly unreadable.

For heaven's sake. She was being an idiot. Of course the barricade had worked; it hadn't even been necessary. Not only had she drunk enough beer to knock out a football team, she'd also passed out. That was enough to kill off any attraction.

And should any lingering tendrils have remained he'd now been treated to her in all her morning glory. A surreptitious glance down showed she was still in the grey top and trousers, now rumpled beyond repair. The strong tea had at least obliterated the fuzzy taste in her mouth, but Olivia could only imagine the state of her face. The remnants of yesterday's make-up; her hair back in bird's-nest mode. So one thing was for sure: any attraction Adam might still have retained for her would have been killed stone-cold dead.

Which was a good thing.

'Good. So now, if you leave me to it, I'll try and transform myself into something more human.'

'OK.' He nodded. 'I'll be in the foyer in half an hour.'

Thirty minutes later she surveyed herself in the mirror. This worked. Cool, calm, and the epitome of poised.

No one would believe the woman in the mirror capable of mad drunken exploits. The navy sleeveless dress had been chosen with a view to impressing Zeb with her professionalism, but it would now hopefully convey to both Adam and Olivia that she was a together person with a mortgage and a business. As opposed to a drunken idiot.

She tugged her freshly washed hair into a high pony-tail, slipped her feet into sensible plain flat navy sandals and made her way out of the bedroom.

Instinctively she turned right and headed towards the foyer, and slowed in an attempt to prepare for the impact of Adam. Now her hangover had receded she could take in his appearance with even more appreciation. Dark hair damp from the shower, a dark green version of the T-shirt that so admirably accentuated his chest, and beige knee-length shorts. Delectable.

But Olivia would be strong.

'Hey,' she said.

'Hey,' he replied.

Dark brown eyes swooped over her body and his lips quirked upward into what really could only be classified as a smirk. As if he knew exactly what her appearance de-noted and thought it was so much hooey.

'So what's the plan for the day?'

'I've got something to show you,' he said.

A boyish smile tilted his lips and against her will her heart did a hop, skip and a jump.

'But first I asked the chef to make you this.' He handed her a plastic container filled to the brim with thick red slush. 'It's a smoothie. Full of dragon fruit and watermelon. There should be enough vitamin C in that to zap the last of your hangover away.'

'Oh…' For an insane second tears prickled the back of her eyes—before common sense asserted itself. It was kind of Adam. Thoughtful of Adam. But it wasn't up there with Mother Teresa. 'Thank you.'

'No problem. Now, let's go.'

Olivia followed him outside, blinking in the brightness as he strode towards the vehicle, his canvas trainers puff-ing up clouds of dust from the path.

Climbing in behind him, she sipped her smoothie and

stared around, marvelling at the scenery, taking in the dark green leaves of the foliage of the palm trees that sprinkled the road. As Adam drove she saw the many scooters that zipped around at seemingly lethal speed and gripped her free hand around her seat belt.

A ten-minute drive and they pulled up outside a secluded villa, set back from the road and nestled within a mini-jungle of lush-leaved plants. Adam jumped down and came round to take her hand—a hand he retained as he led her towards the villa.

Its wooden structure was raised on posts, with an elegantly tapering roof and wide hanging eaves.

'Here we go,' Adam said. 'Our home for the week.'

'You serious?'

'Absolutely. Cooking, cleaning, dusting... Whatever you need doing, I'm your man.'

Whatever she needed? Hauling her mind out of the gutter she stared at him, sensing that for Adam this was a bigger deal than he was letting on.

'Why are you doing this? I have the feeling you want a home like you want a hole in the head.'

'Yeah, well. How much did *you* want to get up on stage and play the drums?'

'That would be hole-in-the-head level.'

'So fair's fair. Plus you issued a challenge—and real men don't refuse a dare.'

'Then lead on, Masterson, and show me the house.'

She followed him towards the front entrance, inhaling the earthy jungle smell of the lush, verdant foliage. 'It belongs to Gan's aunt,' Adam explained. 'She only lets it out to people recommended by Gan because she wants the house to retain its karma.'

Olivia could understand that; there was something personal about the villa that made it different from your average holiday let. Each room was clean and bright, with marble floors cool to the touch of her bare feet. Mismatching mahogany and teak furniture and a variety of Thai statues and tapestries were scattered around. There was also an enormous balcony with a view of the sea that stole her breath, complete with…

'A hammock! Adam, I have *always* wanted a hammock.' She turned to face him. 'Did you choose this place?' she asked. 'Or did Gan tell you about it?'

'I chose it,' he said. 'I saw a few others that were way more luxurious, but this one…well, I thought you'd like it.'

'I do.' But how on earth had he had time to do all this? She glanced at him and then at her watch. 'What time did you get up?'

'Early. Birds and worms and all that.' His expression was closed as he moved towards the sliding balcony door.

Oh, no. Maybe she'd been snoring. Just to add to the drunken, slovenly image. Little wonder if Adam had leapt out of bed and sprinted from the room to find alternative accommodation.

'Well, it was worth it. This place is amazing.' She tipped her palms in the air. 'Who knows? You may love having a home.'

'And maybe pigs will fly.' He smiled, but this time it was that practised smile of charm. 'Let the holiday begin.'

CHAPTER ELEVEN

'ARE WE NEARLY there yet?'

Adam braked to avoid a scooter that had swerved out of nowhere onto the dirt road, then gave Olivia a very swift, fleeting glance from the corner of his eye. 'Seven and a half minutes,' he said.

'Sorry. I'm stupidly excited about these caves. Especially as you won't tell me anything about them *and* you've made me promise not to research them online. So, yes, I am bouncing up and down like an overgrown child. I'll stop now.'

Three days in and this holiday was unlike any Adam had experienced. Truth be told, holidays for a man who had travelled the world and then built up a global empire of hotels had always been problematic.

This time it was different; it couldn't be compared to any of the most decadent, sex-filled sojourns in the penthouse suites of many of his hotels. And surprisingly enough not just because of the lack of any sex—decadent or otherwise.

Because, whilst frustration *was* his constant companion, putting lust aside, Adam was enjoying himself.

No doubt it was the novelty factor, but he loved Olivia's interest in everything—her relish of every bite of food, the way she had spent hours discussing music with Saru, turning his friend into her devoted admirer.

There was also her attitude to both shopping and money. Utterly appreciative when he had held a shop door open for her, she'd bristled into fury when he'd tried to pay for her holiday clothes.

'You're already paying for accommodation and you flew me out here. Our deal doesn't extend to new clothes. In fact I'll pay for *your* clothes. Seeing as I'm making you buy them.'

So for the first time since…well, the first time *ever*… Adam had stood back and watched someone else pull out a credit card. A novel experience, and not one he could see happening again in a hurry. It was hard to imagine his conveyor belt women going Dutch, let alone paying for him. As for purchasing him a selection of slogan-laden T-shirts—one depicting a reggae band, another saying 'Keep Calm and Play the Drums' and another blue number with an underwater sea scene and the caption 'I swim with the fish'—Adam knew that would never happen again, either.

Which was all fine. Predictability and decadent sex was definitely the way forward on future holidays. Unless, of course, frustration killed him first.

He pulled up at the side of the road. 'We're here.'

'And you're sure it's OK for us to do this by ourselves?'

'I'm sure. I know the family who runs the tours. I worked for them as a guide for a whole season, so they know I can do it safely. I've spoken to them. It's all good.'

Though for a moment Adam wondered why on earth he *hadn't* suggested they join a normal tour. Maybe because he wanted to see the wonder on her face when he introduced her to a place that was special to him? He really hoped not. Because that would be worrying. To say nothing of dumb.

A sudden shot of alarm zinged his synapses and he climbed out of the Jeep and inhaled deeply, sucked in the pure forest-scented air as he walked round to open Olivia's door.

He knew exactly what was going on. This was all about the frustration; he wasn't used to spending time with a woman he fancied the pants off and being unable actually to *remove* said pants. So all the lust had nowhere to go and it was affecting his brain. Big time.

Once she'd climbed out he looked her up and down. *Keep it clean, Adam.*

She gusted out a sigh. 'I've got comfortable, sturdy footwear, long sleeves and loose long trousers and I'm smothered in insect repellent. The only way a mozzie will come close to me is if all its nasal tubes have been extracted. Which isn't very likely. So can we go?'

Olivia entered the forest and breathed her appreciation as she looked around the vast canopy of verdant trees. The spectrum of green ranged from vibrant to dark, catching the dappled sunlight so that motes speckled the trailing fronds and leaves.

The path was gentle, almost meandering, and Olivia felt a peace and tranquillity that could only be exploded by... Crashing right bang into Adam's broad back. *Damn.* She'd been trying to hang back; the past few days had shown her all too well the disaster of getting too close. But in her gawping admiration of Mother Nature she'd taken her eye off the ball and now here she was. Back in the danger zone. Up close and personal with the breadth of his shoulders and his scent that won out even over that of the forest.

It took every ounce of her self-control to step backwards—especially as she was sure his body had given a small ripple of appreciation at her touch. *Delusional.*

Adam's face was inscrutable as he indicated what looked to Olivia like a sheer incline.

'Now the climb begins,' he said. 'You ready?'

'Bring it on.'

The harder the better; the more she exerted herself the less she'd desire Adam. That was the theory anyway. But there was something in the thickness of the air, the fertile thriving of this mangrove woodland, that clogged her throat with want.

'Off you go,' he said, and for a second she heard an echo of her own feeling in the depth of his voice. 'I'll be right behind you.'

She was imagining things; she must be. The past few days she'd kept a physical distance, avoided so much as a brush of their hands. As for Adam—Olivia was sure that he no longer wanted her at all. So it must be the magical atmosphere of the forest weaving some sort of hallucinatory spell on her.

Olivia hoisted herself up onto a rock, relieved to see a hanging rope suspended to help her continue the climb up the steep incline. It was an ascent that incorporated not just slippery rock but solid tree branches that jutted out at improbable angles. Thighs aching and calves protesting, Olivia felt sweat sheen her forehead over the twenty minutes it took to reach the cave entrance.

Or at least what Adam called the entrance.

'That's not an entrance. It's a crack in a rock. I'll never fit in there.'

He grinned suddenly. 'Sure you will. You fitted through that window a week ago. I watched you.'

'That feels like a lifetime ago.' Guilt smacked her; a flush rose to her skin. She'd barely given a thought to Zeb or her mum or the baby in the past days. 'Have you heard any news on when Zeb may get here?'

Adam glanced away from her and reached into his rucksack for a bottle of water. 'Gan called earlier. Friends of his met up with Zeb. He should be here tomorrow.'

'Tomorrow?'

Her dismay was embarrassingly apparent and shame coated her as actual disappointment weighed in her tummy. Meeting Zeb was her mission—surely she wasn't shallow enough to care that his arrival heralded the end of their holiday? Even worse, surely it couldn't have anything to do with Adam? She wouldn't, *couldn't* even contemplate that.

'That's great,' she said firmly, and plastered a smile on her face. 'Wonderful.'

'Isn't it?' he agreed, his tone so noncommittal Olivia had no idea what he was thinking. 'But why don't we discuss Zeb later? Negotiating the cave is quite tricky, so it's best if we concentrate on that right now.'

She nodded.

'It's pitch-dark in there, so you'll need this.'

Adam handed her a headlamp and Olivia put it on before watching him angle the breadth of his body into the sliver of darkness between two overhanging rocks.

Sucking her tummy in, she followed, glad of the flashlight as inky darkness enveloped them. The torch illuminated a bamboo ladder leading down into the midnight depths. 'Is there any lighting?' she asked.

'Nope. But your eyes will adjust. Once we get down the ladder make sure you stick close to me.'

'Not a problem.'

A cast-iron excuse to do what she'd longed to do for days, and this time she wasn't going to deny herself. Because tomorrow Zeb would arrive and this whole idyll would end; there would be no more opportunities to be anywhere near Adam after that. The chance of actually acting on this crazy, stupid attraction would definitively be over.

Life would return to normal.

Which was exactly what she wanted. Right? She would have accomplished what she came here for, made an attempt to ensure this baby had a father in his or her life. That was good, right?

Olivia waited for the anticipated buzz of enthusiasm and came up with a flat fizz of two-day-old champagne.

Ridiculous—she was being ridiculous.

'Liv? You OK?'

'I'm fine.' Of course she was. 'I just need to get my bearings.'

Truer words were never spoken.

Once down the ladder she looked round in awe, the light of her headlamp picking out the damp cave walls, the narrow passageways jutted with rocks.

'Follow me, and if you're worried, say,' Adam said. 'It's a bit difficult in places, but I'll be right here every step of the way.'

Olivia bit her lip and nodded. She had to stop reading double meanings into his words but somehow down here, in the very depths of a miracle of nature, every word seemed significant. It felt as though Adam were asking her to follow him somewhere else—or maybe that was wishful thinking on her part. She needed to get a grip; Adam was guiding her through a network of caves, not on some spiritual or sensual journey.

She needed to concentrate or she would fall into the abyss—both literally and metaphorically. Plus, no way should she miss out on an experience like this; these caves were a once in a lifetime... And there went her stupid brain again. Reinterpreting her every thought to bring her back to the idea of sleeping with Adam.

Consigning all such thoughts to perdition, Olivia edged along a bamboo plank, the rush of adrenaline adding to her already skittering nerves. She followed Adam along narrow passageways, scrambled over ancient rocks slippery with underground water and marvelled over a darkness that had never been so much as touched by sunlight.

And all the time the warm bulk of Adam's body both reassured and tantalised her. The whole journey was taking on a hidden depth of meaning as the heavy air of the cave made her dizzy. It wasn't only affecting her, either— she was sure of it. Adam was mostly silent, though always there, steadying her at the exact moment she needed it. But his face, dimly shadowed and dappled by torchlight, held a suppressed urgency, visible in the set of his jaw and the slant of his brows.

'Ooh…' Olivia gasped as she stepped through the narrowest of entrances into a cavernous chamber. It was magnificent; the domed ceilings must have been carved by some god of nature to create such a mystical vault.

Filled with awe, she trailed her fingers along the cold, damp stone.

'Look at these,' she said, and pointed up at the almost implausible stalagmite formations. 'I've never seen anything like them. That shape there—it looks like some sort of guardian…a gargoyle who guards the entrance. They must be ancient.'

Adam nodded. 'I used to stare at them for hours. If you look at them long enough they sizzle your brain.'

Olivia turned to him. 'I thought you were a tour guide.'

'I was. But my first foray into these caves was…' He shrugged. 'Unauthorised. This place—it's a great place to…' He shrugged, rocking back on the balls of his feet. 'Think.'

'I can see that,' Olivia said, and she could—could see an image of a younger, teenaged Adam, all gangly limbs and overlong dark hair, coming to these caves to brood. Perhaps to wish he could stay longer with the people who had been like family to him. Gan, Saru and his parents. That much she'd gleaned from snippets Saru had let slip over the past days—that and the fact that Zeb had been a pretty much absent parent, spending more time in retreat, leaving his son to his own devices until he was ready to move on again.

Olivia gulped, suddenly aware of the sear of his gaze. 'What are you thinking now?'

'You don't want to know.' A rueful smile tugged his lips as he turned his body away. 'Trust me.'

His words echoed through the air, bounced off the strata and into her consciousness. *Trust him.*

Pinning her shoulders back, she sucked in the musky air. 'Actually, I do want to know.'

He swivelled back round on one foot and studied her expression for a long moment. His brown eyes were dark and serious; his face was streaked with loam and age-old grime. 'I was thinking how very much I want you,' he said simply.

'You do?' Encrusted mud dislodged as she raised her eyebrows.

'Yes, Liv, I do. Bit of an open secret.'

Adam's velvet growl smoothed over her skin.

'I thought—' Olivia broke off.

'You thought what?'

'That we were past that. Especially after the other night.'

Adam frowned. 'What happened the other night?'

'Well, I fell asleep in all my clothes and probably snored the night away, the following morning I looked like a cross between a bird's nest and something the cat dragged in, and since then—well, we've shared a house.'

'And sharing a house kills attraction?' He dropped his mouth in mock horror. 'It's because you've seen me wielding a dustpan and brush, isn't it? My macho image is gone for ever.'

Her lips tipped up in a smile. 'Don't be ridiculous. It's me. The last few days I've wandered the house in scruffy pyjamas before I've even brushed my hair. And who knows what I look like now?'

Adam tilted his headlamp and studied her. 'Well, you have clay streaking your cheekbones like some sort of warrior markings and mud smudged across the freckles on your nose.'

'Great! I rest my case. You can't possibly want me looking like this.'

'You don't get it, do you?' He gestured at the air between them. 'This spark we have—it doesn't get cancelled out by tangled hair or rabbit pyjamas or mud. Trust me.'

Those damn words again, echoing round the walls as though the cave itself could pick which words to resonate. *Trust.* She didn't do trust; it wasn't in her make-up or her inclination.

Yet here and now, in this unspoiled place, it was difficult to see anything wrong with a primal, *natural* desire to mate. Adam wanted her and, boy, did she ever want him. Yet…

'We just have to ignore it. Stay in control,' she said, and her words disappeared into the dark currents of air, not deemed worthy of the smallest echo.

Olivia was right. Yet somehow her words didn't tie in with what her whole being was trying to tell him. It seemed clear to Adam that her brain was vying with her body and hanging on by a sliver of fingernail. Perhaps they were both being enchanted by the spirits of the cave? Eternal beings who had lived here for aeons and would be here for centuries more.

OK.

Something was messing with his head.

It was time to take control and regain perspective.

Adam understood exactly why *he* needed to keep the spark between them under control, but it occurred to him that he didn't know why Olivia had pulled back.

He moved towards her, stepping firmly on the slippery rock face.

'Why?' he asked softly. 'Why is it so important to you to not lose control?'

Another step and he was close enough that if she slipped he'd catch her. So near that her scent—loam, clay and that all-elusive apple—taunted him.

'Tell me, Liv.' *Trust me.*

Adam held his breath, lungs aching, not wanting to damage this moment as she hesitated, her teeth caught around her lower lip.

'I won't lose control,' she said. 'Because attraction is all a power game. Two people angling for what they want. Be it sex, money, or the upper hand.'

'You're assuming they are adversaries,' he said gently. 'It doesn't have to be that way.' Something must have happened to make her believe this. 'Did someone hurt you, Olivia? Cheat on you?' His mind scanned for possibilities as he pieced together the fragments she had let fall. 'Someone with money?' The thought of some scumbag breaking her heart and throwing her aside for a newer model balled his fists.

'No.' She shifted her weight and he placed a hand on her arm to steady her, saw indecision pool in her hazel eyes as if in internal debate about confiding in him.

'Why don't we sit down?' he suggested, and led her over the floor towards the corner of the cavern. 'I used to call this The Ledge.' He slipped his rucksack off his shoulder and unzipped it. 'It's where I used to sit and study the stalactites in the hope of achieving hallucinogenic effects.' Rummaging in the bag, he pulled out a waterproof sheet, shook it out and spread it on the ledge. 'Sit down and try it, if you like.'

Olivia sank down lithely and he followed suit, careful to sit close but without touching her. For a long moment she stared at the bulging mass of stalagmites, before clasping her hands on her lap and drawing in an audible breath.

'No one hurt *me*. But my mum—that's a different story.' Hazel eyes met his, clouded with a sadness that twisted his chest. 'When she was fourteen she was raped. By a so-called family friend. She never dared tell anyone.'

Revulsion wrenched Adam's chest, encased his body in steel-cold anger. 'I'm sorry, Olivia.'

'Her life fell apart; she turned into the quintessential rebel. When she was sixteen she met my dad and fell pregnant with me.'

Adam shifted closer to her and took her hand gently in his, and with a small sigh she folded her fingers around his.

'Mum had no qualifications, no family support, but she did have looks and she decided to use them. On her terms. Over the years she had affairs, mostly with rich, married men—men who enjoyed having a gorgeous trophy mistress. That's how we lived.' Her voice caught as she looked at him. 'I vowed that I would not let that happen to me. That I would never depend on anyone for money and I would never let lust control me.' A small shiver ran through her body.

So much made sense now and his heart ached. With Jodie as a tragic example, no wonder Olivia had such mixed feelings about her beauty, about control and power.

Olivia gave a small sniff and pushed away from his chest, swiped her palm across her eyes. 'I shouldn't have told you any of that. It's not fair on Mum.' Her hands clenched into fists. 'I know it looks bad, but I promise she did *not* target your father. I know that, Adam.'

Surprise reared in the hindmost part of his brain, his body stiffening. It hadn't so much as occurred to him to question Olivia's story; it was impossible to suspect that the woman he'd got to know was anything but legitimate.

'It's OK, Liv. *I* believe *you*,' he said. And should her

faith in Jodie prove to be misplaced—because after all they were all human, and old habits died hard—then Adam would not judge Olivia.

In all honesty it wasn't Jodie he was concerned about now—it was Olivia. Because, however cheesy it sounded, this had gone beyond lust; he might not do love or happy-ever-after, but he *wanted* to show her that sex could be a beautiful act between two people. That was well within his remit. They only had one night left. No harm could come of one night.

'I want you to think about something,' he said. 'Zeb arrives tomorrow. What happens after that is out of our control. But until then it's up to you, Olivia. If *you* want to explore this spark more then we can.'

She stared at him, hazel eyes wide. 'Why?' she asked. 'Why have you changed your mind?'

'Because I want to show you that you are a beautiful, desirable woman and that there is nothing wrong with that. I want to show you that losing control can be liberating.'

She shivered and desire flared in her eyes. Adam clenched his hand on his thigh. Because no matter how much he craved to kiss her, taste her, plunder her lush mouth until she felt nothing but burning arousal, this was *her* choice.

'Think about it,' he said, forcing his tone to remain light, as if his entire body *wasn't* seized with need. 'For one day only, I am on offer.'

A small huff of laughter emerged from her lips. 'Are you asking me to step on your conveyor belt for a one-night ride, Masterson?'

'Hell, yes, I am. And it'll be a ride to remember.'

CHAPTER TWELVE

ADAM STOOD ON the villa's balcony and stared out at the glow of the evening sunlight, at the sky streaked with spears of vivid orange as the sun began its glorious descent.

He turned. 'Liv,' he called. 'You're missing the sunset.'

And she loved the sunsets, would gaze mesmerised each evening as if she were etching every colour, every nuance, on the easel of her memory.

'Adam?'

The soft husk of her voice pulled him to the present and he turned away from the pink slivers of disappearing sun.

'Liv... You look—' He broke off and tilted his hands palms-up in the air. 'There are no words.'

The vibrant orange dress she wore was reminiscent of the sunset itself. Its simple off-the-shoulder style bared her sun-kissed skin then cleaved low to reveal the tantalising top of her firm breasts. The clinging material accentuated the slender span of her waist, then dipped to midthigh.

Adam leant against the railings, arms spread, fingers gripping the iron in an attempt to prevent himself from moving forward. His eyes skimmed down the lissom length of her legs, over the toned calves and down to the bejewelled flip-flops that glittered in the rays of the setting sun.

She smiled, her eyes holding a feminine appreciation

of his all too evident male approval. 'I thought we could go out for dinner tonight,' she said. 'On me. I know you can afford a thousand meals, but tonight…it's important to me that I pay.'

'Then I accept, with thanks,' Adam replied, his gaze riveted to her expression. His gut churned in anticipation. Every instinct was telling him that this was it. Olivia had made her decision and tonight would culminate in making all his and her fantasies reality.

Her skin was a touch pale, her oval face framed by the magnificent cascade of strawberry tresses. She wore minimal make-up, so far as he could tell, but her eyelids shimmered and her gorgeous lips were glossy. This was Olivia dressed to kill—and, yes, he was dying over here.

'Where are we going?' he asked, and almost laughed at the deeper meaning under the simple question.

An answering gleam lit her eyes. 'I booked us into Snapper Fish,' she said. 'After that we'll come home.'

And so to bed—or so he hoped. 'Sounds good to me,' he agreed. His gaze lingered on the dress as his brain whirred. 'So that's where you went when we came back? Shopping?'

Olivia nodded. 'I wanted a new dress for the evening. To mark the occasion,' she added with a siren smile.

It was the kind of smile that had his heart threatening to escape his ribcage, the tilt of her glossy lips teasing him.

'Shall we go?' she asked.

Adam nodded; Olivia had a plan and he needed to go along with it. Her choice. Ruining her timetable of seduction—and every atom of his body prayed that he was reading the schedule right—by turning Neanderthal, throwing her over his shoulder and storming to the bedroom, was not an option.

They left the villa and walked in easy silence in the fragrant Ko Lantan dusk. The sweet frangipani-scented air

enveloped them, somehow merging with Olivia's underlying apple scent to send his head awhirl.

The gaily lit restaurant rose out of the dusk and they
followed a waiter onto the covered decking to a secluded
teak table. Amber and orange paper lanterns slanted light
onto the array of floating candles that ornamented the
gleaming wood.

'Good evening, Olivia. Your champagne is on ice, as
requested.'

Olivia nodded. 'Thank you, Kamon.' She turned to
Adam and smiled. 'Thought it would be safer than beer! I
promise not to disgrace myself. And I hope it's OK with
you but I ordered our meal, as well. May as well put all
my research to good use.' She pressed her lips together in
a small smile. 'Sorry. I'm talking too much.'

'I don't mind,' he said. 'I like to hear you talk.'

Dark eyebrows rose as she slid along the wooden bench.
'You do? I kind of thought my chatter would have driven
you nuts by now.'

'Well, you thought wrong.' The sound of her voice, her
sheer enthusiasm and interest in myriad subjects, capti-
vated him. The only thing that might well send him loop-
the-loop would be frustrated desire. If he were reading her
body language all wrong and the evening should culminate in another night alone. But it was Olivia's choice; that
was the deal they had made and he'd honour it. Even at the
cost of his sanity, she had to come to him without regret.

Olivia reached out to the garland of flowers that had
been draped round the edge of the table and smiled.

'I found out some facts about frangipani,' Olivia said.
'Did you know that in different countries they represent
different things? Here in Thailand they were once taboo,
because they were thought to bring sorrow. But now they
are seen as special and worthy of offering to Buddha. In
Vietnam ghosts were thought to live in frangipani trees,

and in India the flower means loyalty.' She rubbed her finger against the petals; the innocent sensuality of the movement constricted his lungs. 'This must have been Kamon's idea,' she said. 'I told him I wanted the dinner to be special.'

Hope and a whole lot more reared its head. 'Any particular reason?' he asked.

Before she could answer, Kamon arrived with a bottle of champagne, two long-stemmed champagne flutes, and an aromatic platter of shrimp tempura. He was followed by another waiter with a further selection of dishes.

The time it took to open the bottle, pour out the fizzing liquid and exchange pleasantries was excruciatingly long. Adam clenched his hands into fists—the only way to stop himself from grabbing the bottle and plate from the obviously besotted Kamon and booting him on his way.

Eventually, after assuring Olivia that everything had been freshly prepared, Kamon wended his way back into the restaurant's interior. Where Adam devoutly hoped he'd stay.

'You didn't hear a word of that, did you?' Olivia asked, a lilt of laughter in her voice.

'Nope.'

'Well, in that case, as penance you'll have to listen to me tell you all about each dish. In detail.'

There was that smile again; pure seduction, it seemed to have a direct line to his pants.

'That's not a problem,' he said. Not if she was going to keep talking with that husk in her voice.

'OK. We have crabmeat and prawn spring rolls with the house special tamarind sauce. Herb-marinated stuffed chicken wings with fragrant lemongrass. Grilled aromatic beef wrapped in betelnut leaves. And lastly honey-marinated duck breast fried in pandan leaf.'

She leant forward in a deliberate movement and Adam nearly bit his tongue.

'Delicious,' he murmured, his eyes fixed without shame on the tops of her firm breasts.

'Then tuck in,' she said.

'I hope to,' he returned, and grinned at the shiver that goosebumped her skin as she hurriedly started to serve herself.

Adam followed suit. It felt good to eat in silence for a while and let the endless possibilities of the night ahead roam free in his brain.

It was only when Olivia gave the characteristic little huff that signified that she was ready to break from eating that he lifted his glass. 'To the rest of our holiday,' he toasted.

Without hesitation she clinked her champagne flute against his, her face glowing in the dappled moonlight just as the overhead lanterns went out.

'Ooh! That means it's time for the fire-dancing,' she said.

For a second Adam wished the dancers would disappear to the Outer Hebrides—before guilt zapped him. Olivia *should* have a chance to see the truly spectacular performance; this was their last night here.

He sipped his drink, the ice cold bubbles focusing him. This night was exactly as it should be. One magical night. And if he had his way the magic would continue straight into the bedroom. He glanced at Olivia, saw the small telltale crease on her forehead, and his gut wrenched at the thought that she might not have made her final decision.

'Oh!' Olivia drew in audible breath as the dancing started. 'How do they *do* that?' she breathed.

The two young Thai men, bare-chested, spun and dipped, twisted and swirled through the shadows of the night. The fire-tipped sticks created incredible patterns that lit up the air with eddies of orange; spirals of flame surrounded each dancer. Olivia gave a small cry and reached out across the table to grab Adam's hand; the heat of her touch on his skin rivalled the blaze of the dance.

'That was incredible,' Olivia breathed.

'They're moving farther down the beach,' Adam said levelly. 'We can go down later and see some more if you like?'

She shook her head, strawberry tresses ruffling round her oval face, releasing the scent of freshly washed hair to tantalise him.

'Crunch time,' she said, letting go of his hand and curling her fingers round the stem of her champagne glass.

Anticipation grapple-hooked his chest, caused his heart to hammer his ribcage.

'I've been thinking about what you said in the cave,' she said. 'About you being on offer for the night.' A small, nervous laugh escaped her lips. 'I've made you sound like a BOGOF supermarket deal.'

Adam tipped his hands upward. 'That doesn't sound like the impression I'm aiming for.' *Keep it light.* Unease prickled his skin at how important Olivia's decision was to him. It was a night. Important? Yes. Crucial to his entire well-being? No. Though it was fast becoming more and more critical to a rapidly growing part of his anatomy.

A welcome smile touched her lips even as she rolled her eyes. 'I was forgetting that you are above the echelons of those needing to shop for bargains. BOGOF means buy one, get one free.'

Adam grinned. 'There's only one of me, honey.'

'Don't I know it? Which is why I've decided to climb on that conveyor belt for the night.'

Relief washed over him in a warm wave even as he strove to remember the rules of the game. 'Welcome aboard.' He sucked in much needed air. 'But remember one thing, Liv. You're unique. Not interchangeable. This night is about *us*. OK?'

She gave a small nod, as if she had processed and approved his words, and then hers lips turned up in a shy smile. 'So what now?'

Adam returned the smile, aiming to project a whole lot of inner wolf. 'We are going to do whatever *you* want, Liv. Your choice. Your control. Your terms.'

Olivia tried to think over the exhilarated buzz that hummed through her body, turning her into a live wire of excitement. They were going to do it—assuage this crazy attraction. Any which way she wanted.

'Whatever I want?' she asked.

He nodded.

'OK. Don't laugh, but I want to go home and sit under the stars and make out.' She blurted the words out.

A smile tipped his lips and creased his eyes.

'Hey,' she protested, 'I said don't laugh.'

'I'm not laughing. I'm thinking that sounds about perfect.'

Light-headedness born of anticipation made her giddy as they rose together. Adam made to pull out his wallet and Olivia shook her head. 'My treat, remember? It's already paid for.'

'So we're all done here?'

'Check.'

'Then come on!'

Olivia's heart did a funny little flip at the huge grin on Adam's face as he held out his hand and she slipped hers into it.

Half running, half walking, both of them laughing in sudden exhilaration, they made it back to the villa. It was only when they stood on the threshold that Olivia felt the onset of faint panic, and an absurd shyness tugged across her chest as they stepped inside.

But diffidence loosened its hold as Adam reclaimed her hand and led the way onto the decking. Without breaking their connection they settled onto the woven bamboo swing chair.

Olivia curled her feet under her bottom on the white cushion as the chair rocked under their weight, feeling that strange shyness returning. It had been easier back in the day in the lift, or in the limo, where passion had simply overtaken them with no time for thought.

This was different. Adam had given her a choice.

She stared up at the inky black sky, coruscating with starlight, and turned to Adam. The half-moon dappled his profile with its beams.

'It's beautiful,' she said, meaning *You're beautiful.* But maybe that wasn't an appropriate thing to say to a man? Her tummy dipped with desire; this was *right.* How could it not be?

Stop overthinking, Liv.

She took a deep breath—infusing her senses with the calming frangipani aroma—and dropped a bare foot to the ground to act as a pivot, twisting herself onto his lap. Her knees straddled his lean hips, the core of her pressed against his hardness, and she exulted in the reaction.

The movement was a deliberate replay of their time in the limo—only this time she knew she wouldn't pull back. She would trust herself to Adam completely.

She pushed her fingers into the thick springiness of his hair and lowered her lips onto his.

As if her actions weren't enough, he growled against her mouth. His lips parted and his tongue touched hers, gently at first, each stroke teasing her, sending a stream of exquisite sensation rollicking through her body.

'More,' she breathed. And with a deep groan he gripped

her waist and rocked against her. Just like that warmth rushed through her lower abdomen and she wriggled in his lap.

Tilting his head, he deepened his kiss, his hands slipping from her waist to plunge downwards and smooth back up her thighs under the skirt of her dress. She writhed to give him room, and when his fingers curved around her bottom and he kneaded the soft flesh she seized in rapture.

Her whole body was alight—until Adam ended their lip-lock. When he pulled back she gave a mewl of protest.

'Liv...' he said, his breathing ragged. 'You need to decide what's next. Because soon we're going to gallop over the line of making out and I won't be able to stop.'

His gorgeous milk chocolate eyes were dark and dilated with raw, primal need and she tensed inwardly, waiting for the automatic reflex of shame. Adam had managed to stop, to call a halt, whereas she would have kept going without a thought. Out of control.

Not so much as a flicker. Instead she felt heady, exhilarated. As if she could swim the Channel doing the butterfly stroke.

Her lips curved upward as she braced her palms against his chest, felt the pounding of his heart beneath her fingers.

'Good,' she whispered. 'Because I don't want you to stop.'

In one lithe movement he stood up, and she wrapped her legs around the solidness of his waist, entwined her arms round his neck as he strode towards the sliding door leading back inside the villa.

She pressed her lips against his, desperate for another of his blissful kisses. Their tongues danced, the tempo increasing as they wended their way through the lounge. Olivia was faintly aware of knick-knacks tumbling in their wake as Adam bumped into a laden table.

They entered the bedroom and Adam halted; Olivia slid down his body and stared up at him, senses awhirl.

She stepped backwards, caught a glimpse of her reflection in the ornate gold-framed mirror. Eyes wide, pupils dilated, a fine sheen of desire glistening in her skin.

She wanted him.

A tight knot of anticipation tangled her tummy up as she slipped her dress off so it fell in a tangerine pool to the floor. She stood in front of him. Just her. Olivia Evans. Completely and utterly naked.

Mouth parched, she licked her lips as her throat clogged in sudden vulnerability. 'Adam…?'

The predatory glint in his eyes as they raked over her said it all. Had more of an effect—she felt hot and squirmy and exultant.

Careful, Olivia. Any beautiful woman standing here would make him react like this.

Really, Liv? You really believe that?

No, she didn't. Because the point was that it *wasn't* any woman standing here. It was her.

'Liv. You are gorgeous.'

He skimmed the back of his finger along her collarbone, followed the curve of her breast until it reached her tight nipple. One soft caress, one light flick with the pad of his thumb, and an electric flash of heat jolted through her body, turning her legs to jelly.

'So beautiful,' he murmured, and for the first time in her life she was glad of it. Wanted to be beautiful, to give pleasure.

'Tell me what you want,' Adam rumbled, the dark chocolate of his voice strumming her skin.

And suddenly it was all so simple 'I want *you*,' she said, and buzzed with exhilaration at the sinful smile that curved his lips and lit his eyes. 'Naked.'

'That's easily arranged.' He crossed his arms, his fingers gripped the bottom edge of his T-shirt and he tugged it over his head.

His chest was perfection: sculpted muscle with a light smattering of hair arrowing down over ripped abs, pointing in a sexy vee towards the ridge in his pants.

'Keep going,' she breathed.

'Patience,' he admonished in a mock growl, before deftly shucking off his shorts and boxers and kicking them unceremoniously to one side.

Holy Moly. Adam was...*magnificent*, was one adjective. *Bloody enormous* would be two.

Mine.

For this night Adam was *hers*.

Her skin felt taut with a yearning to be touched, but her greedy fingers were more interested in him and she wanted to stroke and caress and explore every inch of his muscular glory.

His chest felt hard under her fingertips, and when she smoothed her palms over his hot skin Adam reciprocated, cupping the weight of her breast in his palm, his thumb circling her nipple. Olivia whimpered for more.

Suddenly the backs of her knees hit the edge of the bed and Adam coaxed her down; her back hit the satin coverlet and she looked up at him, braced above her. His palms were either side of her head, his brown eyes so completely focused on her that she shivered from head to foot.

Rolling onto his side, he tiptoed his fingers across her sternum, over her tummy and downward, his eyes hot and heavy with delicious intent as they reached the very heart of her.

His fingers circled and teased and tantalised until she was burning for him, and when he finally slipped inside her she clenched around his fingers. 'Please, Adam,' she breathed, begging him to end the torment.

At her words his erection nudged her thigh and she

reached out to span and stroke the velvety thick length of him. He groaned long and low as she slid her hand to the tip of his hardness, circled the satiny head and glossed over the bead of moisture she found there. He felt amazing.

'You're killing me, Liv,' he gasped.

Not as much as he was killing her.

Olivia undulated on the bed, raised her hips, questing, needing release with a painful intensity as his skilful provoking ministrations pulled her to the brink and back; the pleasure was so excruciating her breath caught in her throat.

Then finally, with one, two, three deft strokes, he found her sweet spot and she cried out, shattered as she clenched around him in release.

It could have been seconds, it could have been minutes before she floated back down to earth to find him watching her, a thoroughly satisfied smile tilting his lips. She stroked his cheek, unable to think of anything to say except thank you—which felt wholly inadequate.

'That was incredible,' she said.

'That's just the starter,' he said. 'You're in luck. It's HOOGOF day.'

'You've lost me.'

'Have one orgasm, get one free,' he murmured, and Olivia burst into a peal of laughter.

'You want to take me up on it?'

'Absolutely, I do.' Hard to believe she could come again, but already her body tingled as he gently nudged her legs apart and knelt between them.

Adam lowered his head to kiss her tummy, then trailed a path of butterfly kisses upwards until he reached her breasts, where he laved first one nipple then the next. Exquisite sensations shot through her, and Olivia gripped his shoulders and scored her nails down the gorgeous supple length of his back.

Waves of pleasure swirled deep inside her and she thrust upward, desperate to have him inside her.

She watched him fist a condom down his length, his hands unsteady. '*Now*, Adam,' she whispered.

Then he was braced above her, sliding that long, hard thickness inside her so slowly that every gorgeous inch sparked a new and building tension, creating a maelstrom of pleasure until she couldn't bear it any more.

'Please...' she moaned, and he began to thrust faster, harder, the sensuous wonder so fierce Olivia thought she'd pass out. Then they reached the apex and she shattered beneath him, crying out his name as she soared to release. Distantly she heard Adam's deep, exultant roar and knew he'd followed her into the abyss.

Olivia opened her eyes to the lilting sound of birdsong and the knowledge that all was right in the world. A world where she lay cocooned in Adam's strong embrace, enclaved in a sanctuary of sheer bliss.

The night and the pre-dawn hours had fulfilled and exceeded any flight of fantasy, and had revealed to her a truth so blinding in its pure simplicity that she felt like an idiot for never realising it before.

Yet at a primal level she knew no one else could have shown her except Adam. He had demonstrated that a union of bodies was exactly that. A union. She and Adam had given and taken, shared a mingling of mutual need and fulfilment, soared on the waves of ecstasy to achieve communion.

Nothing she had experienced before could be compared—no more than she would liken the flickering light of a nearly dead torch to the hot blaze of a desert sun.

Very gently she shifted, not wanting to wake Adam but consumed by the need to see him, to study the planes and angles of his sleeping face. Too late; his eyes had opened and he surveyed her with drowsy, languorous contentment.

'Hey,' he said, and his sleep-roughened voice tugged her heart as he pulled the blanket over his head and pulled her back into the crook of his arm.

A sudden realisation shot through Olivia: she would never see him like this again. Dark hair mussed from her fingers, bare, smooth skin available for her caress. Never again would Olivia experience the magic of their bodies' union.

Zeb was arriving; the night was over. The portals of paradise were swinging closed and reality had to be faced. The irony of the situation struck her. A week ago all she had wanted was to locate Zeb Masterson. Now she wished she could put off his arrival for just one more day.

But that wasn't possible, so somehow she had to be all right. She'd known the rules—could hardly cavil now. Yet Adam had changed so much in her life. He'd smashed her notions of desire; he had shown her that a man could still desire a woman even if she didn't look perfect all the time. That sex could be a beautiful, consensual act, and that a little bit of power play could be fun. As long as there was trust.

That was it. Somehow over the past week she'd grown to trust him, to believe that he saw her as a unique individual and not a beautiful commodity.

And if he had changed *her* so fundamentally then maybe there was a chance that she had done the same for him. Turned his conveyor belt view of relationships topsy-turvy?

A furling tendril of hope took root. Later, after they had seen Zeb, she would talk to Adam. After all, there was nothing to stop them from exploring their feelings. This baby could be a shared bond between them; it didn't have to be a barrier.

Drowsily Olivia closed her eyes....

She woke later to the aroma of coffee teasing her nostrils and the realisation that Adam was no longer next to her.

No need to panic.

Today was about meeting Zeb. It was time for her to put all these new burgeoning feelings aside and focus on the baby. No way could she tell Adam anything about her epiphany. *Yet.*

CHAPTER THIRTEEN

ADAM DROPPED WATERMELON slices into the juicer and pushed the on button. Soon enough all these oddly domestic chores would end. No more preparing breakfast, or visiting the market for ingredients, or cooking with Olivia.

In fact reality dictated that within hours they might well be on their way back to the UK. Mission accomplished.

And it wasn't only household activities that would cease; there would be no more shared bedroom antics, either. His body gave a cold shiver that belied the blazing sunshine pouring through the open window. The shudder of protest was augmented by the fire of memory from the night before; his mind and body were still caught up in the flow and eddy of the most amazing sensual experience of his life.

He'd known that he and Olivia had a spark; he'd failed to realise it would be an ember that lit flames so intense he doubted they would ever bank.

Whatever they had shared last night had transcended sex; there had been a connection, a mutual bond that sent a bolt of panic straight down his spine. Definitely time to call it a day. He'd waded into the pots and pans, scrubbed a few floors. and now it was time to play the 'I'm a billionaire, get me out of here' card.

'How do I look?'

Olivia's soft voice broke his reverie and he turned from the kitchen counter.

His breath hitched in his throat; she was stunning.

She wore a fluorescent camisole top over white jeans, a jewelled clip held her hair in a knot on the top of her head, strawberry blonde tendrils escaped to frame her sun-kissed face.

A far cry from the muted dressed-in-grey girl who had arrived on Ko Lanta in her carefully chosen neutral outfit to meet Zeb.

This Olivia would meet Zeb on her own terms—as herself.

'You look perfect,' he said simply as he handed her a glass of smoothie.

'Thank you.' Sipping the vivid red drink, she shifted from foot to foot. 'So where are we meeting him?'

'Gan is taking him to Saru's bar. They should be getting there any minute now.'

'How are you feeling?' she asked.

A daft glow lit deep within him because she cared, even as instinct told him to dodge the question. This wasn't about him, and nor did he want to discuss Zeb in arbitrary detail. This new chapter in Zeb's life should not be influenced by the old.

'Fine,' he said.

Her lips pouted in a plump moue of disbelief. 'I want to know how you're *really* feeling.'

Trying not to focus on the mouth that had moved over his body with such devastating effect only hours ago, he hitched his shoulders. 'I'm not feeling anything. Best not to with Zeb, because you never know what to expect.'

'So there is no point having expectations?' she said softly as she moved towards him, surrounded him with a cloud of sheer Olivia. 'Does he know we're here?'

'He knows *I'm* here. But that's no guarantee that he'll

stick around. Zeb has a good nose for danger. He'll suspect that it has to be something pretty big to get me out here waiting for him for a week. So the sooner we get to him the better. But first tell me how *you're* feeling.'

'Nervous. I hope with all my heart that Zeb will step up and want to be a great father.' She wrapped a stray tendril of hair around her finger. 'But no matter what happens now, this week has been incredible.'

Suspicion pricked his thumbs; there was something in Olivia's expressive eyes that initiated unease. Ridiculous. Adam shoved the brooding thought aside. They had an agreement: one night. Olivia knew and concurred with the rules—and anyway she didn't believe in love and wasn't looking for a relationship.

Whatever bond had been formed would now be dissolved. Following this meeting with Zeb, he and Olivia would go their separate ways. If Zeb confirmed paternity then perhaps their paths would occasionally cross and the steeped banks of desire would give a little smoulder. But right now she deserved his support; she must be anxious about Zeb. *That* was the vibe he was picking up.

'Come on.' He held out his hand and braced himself for the shock of impact. This was a grasp of friendship, nothing more. 'Let's do this.'

Her small decisive nod betokened determination and she slipped her hand into his.

A ten-minute Jeep drive brought them to their destination and after a brief beach walk they stepped out of the bright morning sunlight into the cool interior of the bar. Adam scanned the room; only a few tables were occupied, and the muted hum of conversation blended with the low background beat of reggae music.

There was Zeb, and the familiar conflicted jumble of feelings knotted in Adam's gut. The leaden knowledge that this was the man who had moulded him genetically and by nurture had made him, for better or worse, into the man he was today. A massive chunk off the old block. Then there was gratitude that Zeb had done his duty, had swooped in to rescue Adam from the terror of the care system. And of course the thread of guilt that his father's much wanted arrival had come at the cost of his mother's death.

Too many emotions, added to the tumult of feelings generated by Olivia—who was rigid by his side as she stared at Zeb.

'Hey. It's going to be all right. We can do this,' he said, hoping it wasn't the biggest lie ever.

'OK…' she whispered.

They walked towards the table and Zeb looked up, his brown eyes glinting from Adam and then resting on Olivia.

'Adam. My boy. How's the hotel business?' The question was a standard one, the reply never listened to. 'More important, who is *this*?' Zeb turned directly to Olivia and stroked his chin. 'Whoever you are, you look familiar.'

'This is Olivia,' Adam said. 'Olivia, this is Zeb.'

Olivia stepped forward and leant across the table. 'I'm Jodie's daughter.'

For an agonising second a pang of guilt by association burned Adam's neck. He prayed that his father remembered Jodie—hadn't dismissed her from memory once she'd stepped off Zeb's conveyor belt.

'Hawaii,' Adam prompted.

'Of course.' Zeb nodded. 'Apologies, Olivia. Your mother seemed way too young to have a daughter your age, hence the confusion. Hawaii. What a wonderful place, as Adam can no doubt tell you. Sit down, both of you. I'm having a rather marvellous cocktail. Five days at sea on basic provisions, cleansing my body and soul, and I feel ready for one of these. Can I get you one?'

'No, thank you.' Olivia's opened her mouth to continue,

her expression glazed; no doubt she was looking for a polite way to turn the conversation.

Before she could utter a word Zeb launched into a lecture on cocktails of the world. Adam recognised the tactic all too well. Heaven help him, it was a strategy *he* had utilised in many a business meeting.

Behind the façade of bonhomie, even as his mouth poured forth a torrent of avuncular chat, Zeb's brain would be working overtime. Assessing and discarding the possible reasons for Olivia's presence in the same way he would evaluate the cards in a hand at a game of poker.

It was entirely feasible that any minute now Zeb would guess and quite simply do a runner before Olivia could break the news.

Adam moved to sit at the table, positioning himself between Zeb and the door. He wouldn't interfere in the conversation unless it became imperative, but neither would he let Zeb leave without being told about the baby.

After all, who knew? Maybe this time around Zeb would welcome impending fatherhood. Olivia's optimism might be well founded; no one was asking Zeb to be a single parent again. Olivia just wanted him to be a part of the baby's life. Surely *that* wouldn't cramp Zeb's style?

'So...' Olivia managed, slipping onto the seat next to Adam. 'Did you and my mother have any cocktails in Hawaii?'

'Ah, yes. Hawaii. I got distracted. Definitely an excellent place to holiday.'

'So *my mother* said.'

Zeb looked disconcerted, but only for a second. 'Indeed. And how *is* your beautiful mother? Do give her my best and...'

For goodness' sake.

Impatience snapped within Adam and he opened his mouth to intervene just as Olivia leant forward and thumped the table. Her small fist caused the cocktail to give a little jump, its paper umbrella falling to the tabletop.

'Jodie is pregnant,' she stated. 'And you're the father.'

Pallor stripped Zeb's face of its tan and rendered it blotchy. With one abrupt move he snatched the glass and drained it, before signalling to Saru for another one.

'Are you sure?' he demanded, all trace of bluff joviality vanishing

'Yes.'

'So why isn't Jodie here?' Zeb asked.

'Because she believes that you won't want to know; she thinks it's unfair to burden you with a child you hadn't bargained for.'

The colour returned to Zeb's face, along with a smile that creased his eyes but didn't reach it. 'Your mother is a wise lady,' he said.

As the impact of Zeb's words smashed into him Adam shifted his chair closer to Olivia and laid a hand on her denim-clad thigh. Anger and sadness vied inside him; clearly being a father to Adam had changed nothing for Zeb.

'Yes, she is,' Olivia said quietly. 'But I still thought that you would want to know. That you'd want to be a part of your baby's life.'

Saru brought the drink across; as he placed it in front of Zeb he shot Adam a quick glance. Instead of returning to the bar he sauntered towards the door, seemingly casually, effectively blocking Zeb's exit.

'It's better if I'm not,' Zeb said. 'I'm sure Adam has told you that I'm a wanderer. I'm not parent material. I've done my parenting stint and it's over. Of course I can send money—or if I can't Adam certainly can.' Zeb pushed his chair back and made to rise. 'Be sure to wish Jodie well.'

'Wait.' Olivia's voice was sharp. 'Please.'

'My dear girl, there is little point in trying to change my mind.'

Zeb stood and Adam mirrored the action.

'Sit,' he said. 'Olivia wants you to stay, so that is what is happening.'

Zeb hesitated and then threw his hands in the air. 'Very well, then.' He sank back down with a shake of his greying head.

'Don't you feel *anything* for your baby?' Olivia asked.

Adam flinched, wondering if Olivia was thinking of her own father. This must be her personal hell: to see the face of indifference in the flesh. Here was a man thinking only of himself, with never a thought for the child he had helped create.

'Of course I feel something,' Zeb said expansively. 'I accept a fiscal responsibility and I believe that I am doing the right thing for the child. Better that I don't raise any expectations that I know all too well I cannot come anywhere near fulfilling. The Mastersons don't like to be tied down, Olivia.' He waved a hand at Adam. 'Adam will vouch for that.'

Zeb's words sucker-punched Adam. They were no more than the truth and he would do well to remember it.

'So...' Zeb picked up his drink and glugged it down. 'Any more questions? Do I need to order another drink or am I free to go?'

Adam shot a glance at Olivia, who shook her head. She looked pale, her shoulders slumped, and his heart ached for her. For a second he was tempted to grab Zeb and force him to do what she wanted, make him grovel to Olivia for hurting her. But there was no use in walking that path. It would simply put off the inevitable. Zeb would always leave; that was what Mastersons did.

'Just go, Zeb.'

Weariness descended on Adam's shoulders as he watched Zeb bound to his feet.

For a second the older man hesitated. 'Adam, I am as I am.' He walked around the table and clapped an awkward hand on Adam's shoulder. 'I'll see you.' He nodded towards the door. 'You may want to let your friends know I'm good to go.'

Adam turned and nodded at Saru, knowing he'd pass the signal onto Gan, who was no doubt lurking in the vicinity.

'Ciao.'

With that, Zeb was gone.

'Olivia.' Despite knowing Zeb's actions weren't his fault, guilt jabbed at Adam. 'I'm sorry.'

She expelled a sigh and shook her head. 'Don't be. You didn't walk out through that door. I just can't believe that's how it went down.'

She reached across the table and picked up the paper umbrella, closing it carefully, smoothing the thin paper folds.

'I played it wrong. I should have tried harder. Asked more questions. Told him more about Mum. I should have done *something*. Asked you and Saru to keep him here locked up. Instead I let him leave.'

'It wasn't your fault.'

'Easy for you to say. *I'm* the one who stuffed it up.'

'You didn't stuff it up. Leaving is what Zeb does.'

No one knew that better than Adam, and he needed Olivia to believe that. To stop blaming herself.

'What do you mean?'

'I mean Zeb called it right. Mastersons aren't good at being tied down. There is nothing you can say or do to change that.'

'He looked after *you*,' Olivia said softly.

'Reluctantly.' The dark twist of knowledge wrenched

his insides. 'He looked into every other avenue first and he cut me loose at the first opportunity.'

'I don't understand.'

Adam ran a hand down his face and round the back of his neck; memory's bitter taste coated his very soul. A memory he'd never shared with anyone.

But here and now he could not let Olivia think that if she'd done something differently Zeb would have made a different decision. He'd hoped for her sake that Zeb would. Hell, he'd hoped it for his own sake. Wished that having Adam in his life, being a parent, had affected Zeb in some way. Clearly not. And Adam could see now what a foolish mirage *that* had been.

'It was my sixteenth birthday and we were celebrating.' Adam had been stupidly pleased; it had been the first time Zeb had marked his birthday in any way. 'Turned out we weren't celebrating my birthday.'

'What do you mean?'

'It was my send-off party.' He could feel the weight of Zeb's hand on his shoulder, hear his voice echo down the twelve years.

'You're old enough to fend for yourself.'

'I don't get it, Zeb. What does that mean?'

Zeb raised his champagne glass. 'Son, I'll be honest with you. Having a kid around is kind of cramping my style. I've done my duty by you and now it's time to cut you loose.' A hearty slap on the back. 'But no worries. We'll keep in touch.'

Then, 'Ciao!' and he'd upped and gone.

'But… That's awful,' Olivia whispered after Adam had given her a shortened version of their exchange.

'Zeb never wanted to be a father. But he did step up to bat when there was no other choice. I guess to him it seemed the right thing to do. He put in an eight-year sentence and figured he'd paid his debt to parenthood.'

'That sucks. It really sucks, Adam.' She shook her head. 'You should have told me.'

'Not fair. Zeb's relationship with me shouldn't have prejudiced you. Maybe if I'd been a different type of son things would have been different. It could have been he'd changed his opinion on parenthood over the past fourteen years.'

Foolish thoughts, really; Mastersons didn't change their spots.

Olivia stared down at the table and then whipped her head up, nostrils flaring. 'Then the baby is better off without him.' She swept a sideways glance at him. 'And so are you. Kudos to you. Zeb cut you loose and you forged a great life for yourself.'

Typical Olivia. Even in her own hurt she could find time to try and make him feel better. The least he could do was reciprocate in kind, with the truth. 'So will this baby. He or she will have you and that will make all the difference.'

She shook her head. 'No. It's Jodie who'll do that. I'll just do my best to help. Now I know the score, I need to get home and tell her.'

'You can fly back in the jet. Tell me when you want to go. I'll let the pilot know.'

'What about you?' Olivia asked.

'I'm going to stay in Thailand. Move around. Research some hotel options—maybe design a more "homey" type of hotel. With alphabetical spices.' The smile he could always summon at will just this once refused to comply. 'But I can ferry you across to the mainland today, if you're in a hurry to get back.'

Olivia's heart plummeted; it seemed more than clear that Adam was dead set on getting rid of her, *pronto*.

Perhaps she should go. After all, didn't Adam keep saying that he was a chip off the old block? And she'd just seen the old block in action. *No.* Adam wasn't like that. This she knew with a bone-deep certainty.

Pulling her shoulders back, she stood up to face him. 'That's really kind of you. But before you do that I'd like to talk. We haven't had a chance since last night, and… and so much has happened in the last twelve hours and… and… We need to talk.'

Colour angled over his cheekbones, though she wasn't sure if it was a flush of embarrassment or sheer irritation at her presumptuousness. Maybe conveyor belt women didn't require conversation. *Well, tough.*

'Of course,' he said. 'Why don't we sit out on the beach for a while?'

'Good idea.' Somehow it seemed preferable to have this discussion in the open air, with only the sea and sand as witness.

She blinked as they exited the bar; the dazzling sparkle of light hazed the sand golden, the soft grains scrunching under her toes. Adam maintained a distance, his hands jammed in his chino pockets, his withdrawal from her complete.

Hard to reconcile this grim man with *her* Adam, who had transported her to such heights of ecstasy.

They reached the edge of the sand and Olivia kept going into the waves, let the sun-warmed turquoise water wash over her toes. She stared out at the timeless horizon of blue, its brightness so intense, so still, it almost overwhelmed her. The blue of the cloudless sky was undisturbed by the swoop of even a solitary bird.

No courage to be found there; that would have to be dredged from somewhere within her, nurtured by the memory of what she and Adam had shared these past days. Their shared laughter and relaxed silences, their animated conversations about everything and nothing. The mind-blowing, incredible union of their bodies.

Turning, she moved towards him. He sat, long legs stretched out, palms down in the sand to brace his weight.

She sank down next to him, the heat of the sand permeating the white denim of her jeans, and pulled her knees up, hugging them to her.

'I—' She broke off. Where to begin? Maybe best to cut to the chase. Roll the dice…show her hand. 'I want to change the rules.'

His head snapped round with neck-cricking speed. 'Excuse me?'

'I'd like us to see each other again. Not as fling partners but as…'

'As what?' His voice was hoarse; the words rasped from his throat.

Olivia dug her fingers into the sand. 'As two people who want to spend time together and see what happens.'

A derisive snort indicated his opinion. 'I can tell you what would happen.'

'What? Suddenly you're the Delphi Oracle? You can't know what would happen.'

'Yes, I can. Someone would get hurt. Olivia.'

Not *Liv* any more—and, wow, that did hurt.

'It doesn't have to be like that.' Shifting in the sand, she wanted to reach out, but couldn't. She was too sure that he would flinch, and that would suck away the last bit of her courage. 'You've made me see that. A relationship doesn't have to be a power game. It can be a partnership, a give and take.'

His whole body stiffened, tension visibly rippling across his shoulderblades. 'You're mixing up a relationship with sex. We had crazy hot sex. That doesn't make a relationship.'

'We had more than that, Adam, and you know it.'

'In which case all the better to end it here and now.' Rooting in the sand, he pulled out a smooth, round stone and with a deft, angry flick of his wrist sent it cresting across the waves.

Olivia watched the pebble hop, skip, and jump before sinking into the watery depths. Indicative of where this conversation was going.

'Why?' she asked. 'Why won't you give us a chance to become something more? At least tell me that. Did I read it wrong?'

He twisted his torso and made a guttural sound, reminiscent of pain. 'You did nothing wrong, Olivia. It's me. I'm not relationship material. You just met Zeb—surely that gave you a clue?'

'You are not like Zeb,' If only she could get that through his thick, stubborn skull.

'I'm a carbon bloody copy.'

'That's not true. It doesn't even make sense. You're you. You make your own choices.'

'I do. And I choose to not hurt anyone else.'

He must be talking about his ex-wife. 'Did you hurt Charlotte?'

'Yes.' He uttered the syllable with a savage twist of self-derision. 'I married her and then two years later I left her.'

'Relationships break down. It happens.'

'Our marriage didn't break down, Olivia. I destroyed it. I promised Charlotte everything. A white picket fence, a family—the whole deal. When push came to shove I couldn't make good. It's the only deal I ever reneged on in my life.'

His large body was still rigid with a tautness she longed to soothe. The knowledge that he would reject her touch caused her to bury her hands in the warmth of the sand.

'What happened?' she asked instead.

'I blew it. Because every day the walls closed in a little more. I threw myself into work—anything to avoid returning to a place that had become like a prison. Eventually

I couldn't take it any more. So in true Masterson style I upped and left. I vowed to give Charlotte the rest of my life and I managed less than eight hundred days before I cracked and walked out of the door. Just like Zeb walked out of Saru's.'

His voice was so full of self-derision, so sure of his own guilt, it turned her thoughts topsy-turvy.

'So that's why we cannot take this any further. I hurt one woman in the pursuit of an impossible dream. I won't hurt another. You deserve better. A man who wants a home and a family. A man you can trust.'

His last five words stopped her in her tracks. Adam was right. If they took things further they would spend the whole time waiting for the sword to fall. Damocles would have nothing on them. Olivia loved her home; the thought of sitting in it, waiting and watching to see the walls close in on Adam, made her body shiver in revolt. All they could have was an interval until Adam left.

She had just witnessed what an utter coward Zeb was, and it was Zeb who had brought Adam up—Zeb whose genes he carried. Which explained why Adam still moved from place to place, had his moving line of beautiful women. What an idiot she was; she'd let mind-blowing sex blind her to all common sense. Looked through the filter of an amazing orgasm or three and made herself believe that Adam Masterson was something he wasn't.

Been willing to take a risk and trust him, let him in to her carefully constructed life. She couldn't even blame *him*—after all, Adam had never lied to her; he knew the kind of man he was and acknowledged it freely. He was a man who walked away. Like his father. Like her own father.

Idiot didn't begin to cover it. Because she'd broken all her own rules and now her poor exposed heart was shattering.

But, damn it, she'd chosen to jump on the conveyor belt and now she would climb off with her dignity and her self-respect intact. Hell, she'd even take him up on the private jet offer.

She gulped in the salty air before rising to her feet. 'You're right. I do deserve all of that. So if you wouldn't mind sorting out the jet I'll go back and pack. I can get a boat to the mainland, then a taxi to the airport—or I'm sure Gan or Saru would drive me. Good luck, Adam. And thanks for last night—it was fun. But you're right. Better to quit whilst we're ahead of the game.'

Turning, she walked away across the sand and didn't look back.

Didn't see Adam scramble to his feet and stretch out a hand.

Didn't hear his whispered, 'Liv...' before he slammed his hands into his pockets and stared out to sea.

CHAPTER FOURTEEN

OLIVIA DUCT-TAPED the cardboard box securely and hoisted herself up from her hunched crouch. Pressing one hand to the small of her back, she stretched and glanced around the packing-case-strewn floor of her mum's apartment.

'We're getting there,' she said, watching as Jodie carefully wrapped a delicate glass figurine in tissue paper.

Jodie smiled at her. 'And we'd get there a lot quicker if you stopped clucking over me and let me do more.'

'You've done loads. And you're six months pregnant, remember?'

'Well, second trimester or not, I can make my lovely daughter a cup of tea.'

'Thank you, Mum.'

Jodie glided across the thick-pile cream carpet, one hand circling her swollen belly with a reverent touch that filled Olivia with a strange yearning. Admiration and love mingled in her chest. Her mother had been completely unfazed by Zeb's attitude—had accepted his decision with a serene dignity. She hadn't let it affect her enjoyment in her pregnancy. Diet, yoga—anything Jodie could do to ensure the health of the baby she was doing. In spades.

'This way the baby will be healthy and so will I,' she'd explained. 'So I can look after her properly.' Reaching out, she'd laid a hand on Olivia's forearm. 'I know I made mistakes with you, Livvy. I want to make sure this time I get it right.'

'Oh, Mum. You did great with me. I couldn't have wished for a better mum.'

'That's sweet of you, darling, even if it's the most enormous fib. I do know that I love you more than anything else in my life. But it's time I stopped relying on you. This baby is a second chance for me. I have to learn to stand on my own two feet.' Jodie lifted an elegant hand to forestall Olivia's protest. 'It's true. I'm forty-two years old and I have spent my whole life depending on other people. I owe you an apology.'

'No. You don't.'

'Yes, I do. I am determined things are going to change. I've even got myself a job in the mother and baby store in town, and I love it.'

And over the two months since Olivia's return from the disastrous Masterson Mission she had come to see that Jodie meant every word.

Memories threatened. Adam's sinful smile—the real one that she had believed was for her and her alone. His eyes—shades of brown, glinting with mischief or dark with desire. His touch. When would her body stop craving it?

'Livvy? Tea's up.'

Olivia blinked the thoughts away and focused on the present, accepted the steaming mug with an attempt at a smile. She needed to banish Adam from her brain or at least wean herself off the man. Allow herself a hundred memories today and ninety-nine tomorrow.

Her mum's blue eyes studied her way too thoughtfully.

'How did last night go?' Olivia blurted. 'At antenatal class? I'm so sorry I couldn't make it, but—'

'Sweetheart, I told you—it's fine. I get that you needed

to see a client. It's no biggie. The class went well. Really well, in fact.'

Jodie opened her mouth and then closed it again, turned away so that her highlighted bob swung forward to hide her expression.

'Mum, are you sure everything is OK? You *do* know you don't have to move out of here?'

Jodie swung back round. 'Olivia Louisa Evans. We are *not* having this conversation again. I am appalled with myself for not realising long ago how wrong it was that you have been paying the extortionate rent on this place.' Her lips curved into a loving smile. 'Plus, I adore my new place. It's way more suitable for Bubs and me. There's a park. Local shops. It's a real community. Anyway, you're still contributing to the rent.'

'Mum. I've explained. I'm not *contributing.* You're earning the money. Consulting at Working Wardrobes counts as a job.'

It had turned out that whilst Olivia had been away her stand-in had gone AWOL. It had been Jodie who had stepped into the breach; Suzi, love her, had the clothes sense of a horse.

Her mother had done an amazing job.

There came a lash of guilt. If Jodie had been wrong to accept Olivia's help, Olivia had been wrong not to be honest with her mother. Had been wrong in so many of the assumptions she had made about Jodie. Turned out some people *did* change.

'Where are you going?' she asked as Jodie shrugged herself into her chic lime-green raincoat.

'Milk,' Jodie said. 'I've run out of milk. I'll just pop out.'

'I can go.'

'No. It's good exercise for me.' Jodie tied the belt loosely around her waist. 'See you later, Livvy.'

Five minutes after the door had clicked shut behind her mum the doorbell chimed. Sighing, Olivia switched the Hoover off. Many things had changed about Jodie, but housework still wasn't her forte. There was enough dust gathered behind the sofa to fill a skip. Olivia swiped a hand across her brow and grimaced as she glanced in the mirror. The postman was in for a bit of a shock.

She pulled the door open and shock impacted her, dropped her chin kneewards. 'What are you—?'

And why now? If ever she had been stupid enough to hallucinate Adam turning up unannounced, the vision had *not* included Olivia dressed in an old apron, with a scarf over her head, looking like a demented version of a fifties housewife.

Deep breath.

'Adam. What are you doing here?' She half closed the door and stepped forward, holding the handle behind her back.

'I'm here to see you. Didn't Jodie mention it?'

Just great. Maybe her mum was retaliating against Olivia's foolhardy jaunt across the world to find a man her mother had already identified as a waste of space.

'No. She didn't mention it.'

'Ah. Well, she knows I'm here. So can I come in?'

'No.' Just this glimpse of him was half killing her; no way was she letting him inside.

Dark blue jeans moulded to muscular thighs, and his reggae T-shirt stretched across the expanse of his chest and brought back a flood of memories she'd kept at bay for weeks. His dark hair was longer than she remembered, and it glinted with raindrops from the intermittent spring showers that were plaguing Bath.

Adam sighed. 'I'm not going anywhere, Olivia. So you have two choices. You can let me in. Or I can pick you up, sling you over my shoulder and carry you inside. Your choice. Three seconds.'

For an insane heartbeat Olivia was tempted to hold her ground; a tremor weakened her legs at the thought of being thrown over Adam's shoulder.

As if reading her mind, he raised an eyebrow and stepped forward.

She had to get a grip; if she let Adam touch her she would be lost. Stepping backwards, she sucked in a breath to avoid any such possibility. The downside of that strategy being that she got a lungful of his woodsy scent. Her head whirled as desire jolted through her.

'Let's make this quick. I don't care if Mum knows you're here. I want you gone before she gets back.'

'That's no problem. Jodie won't be back for a while.'

'Huh? What have you done? Where is she?'

'Liv, I'm not the mafia, and this isn't a mob movie. Jodie said she'd spend the day with her friend Juliette and go to the cinema.'

He'd called her Liv, and the fact spread warmth over her chest. A heat she had to fight.

'Hang on a minute.' Olivia slammed her hands onto her hips, tried to ignore the sudden predatory glint in his eyes as they rested on her body. 'Exactly when did Mum tell you all of this?'

'Yesterday. I called her and we met for a coffee. Or a herbal tea, in your mum's case.'

'You came to sort out the money?' Why else would he have turned up?

'Amongst other things,' he agreed calmly. 'Your mother strikes a hard bargain.'

'She took the money?' Confusion mixed with an obscure sense of disappointment.

'Why shouldn't she? The baby is my sister just as much as yours. I don't see why she shouldn't benefit. Jodie suggested I set up a trust fund for the baby, which is exactly what I've done. The money will be hers when she reaches the age of twenty-one—or before, if Jodie, you and I all agree. So if she wants to go to university, or go travelling, or set up a business, or buy a home she'll be able to.'

Adam smiled. *Her* smile—the one that warmed his eyes and curled her toes in the grubby trainers that currently adorned her feet.

'You and your mum are very alike. It took me a while to persuade her to accept anything from me.'

Olivia flexed her feet and attempted to pull her brain into gear. 'This is all very generous of you, Adam, but it's between you and Mum. Nothing to do with me. It doesn't explain why you're here. Unless you want my gratitude? If so, thanks very much, and the door is that way.'

Ungracious, she knew. But Adam must know that she couldn't be bought—though what he was trying to buy was anyone's guess. Another night? Heaven help her, her body melted at the thought. So the sooner he left, the better.

He stepped forwards, closing the space between them, and she moved backwards, manoeuvred herself behind the sofa.

'I'm not after your gratitude, Liv. I came here because I wanted to see you. I *needed* to see you.'

Her tummy fluttered with an anticipatory fizz that common sense instantly doused. There were loads of reasons for Adam to need to see her. She tucked a stray tendril of hair behind her ear, her fingers skimming the synthetic material of the utterly horrendous scarf. Her fingers itched with the feminine need to tug the damn thing off and she dropped her hands to grip the back of the sofa. She didn't care how she looked.

'If you need me to sign something to do with the trust fund leave the papers here. I'll get them back to you once I've read them.'

'That's not what I need.' Brown eyes looked at her with a hunger he made no effort to hide. 'Why didn't you tell your mum about us?'

Olivia narrowed her eyes. 'How do you know I didn't?'

'Because after I took her to her antenatal class last night we went for a drink, and until I explained the situation she seemed to think that I was just someone who'd helped you find Zeb.'

Olivia wasn't sure which bit of the sentence to tackle first. 'You went to her antenatal class?'

'Yes.'

Adam took another step closer to the sofa so that he stood at the corner, and her heart started flipping like a blueberry pancake in her chest.

'Why?'

'Because I want to be part of my sister's life.'

'You do?'

'Yes,' he said simply. 'Just because Zeb isn't choosing to feature it doesn't mean I can't. That's why I went to Jodie first, before coming to find you. I want you both to know that regardless of what happens between you and me I will always be involved. Not out of duty but out of love.'

His words swam around her mind, her brain circling and trying to come to terms with them. It focused finally on 'regardless of what happens between you and me'.

'You and me?' Clenching her nails into the palms of her hand, she straightened her shoulders. 'I don't understand. There *is* no you and me. And, whatever happened between us in the past, I'd never stand in the way of you being in the baby's life.'

'I want there to be a you and me.'

His words resurrected that tendril of hope—the very one she thought she'd uprooted and composted. *Careful, Olivia.* He'd cracked her barriers and her heart on a Thai beach two months ago. *Don't let him hurt you more.*

'You were pretty damn clear two months ago that that wasn't a possibility. Sure enough that you convinced me.'

He rubbed a hand over his face and back up and through his hair—such a familiar gesture that her heart ached.

'Two months ago I was an idiot.'

'And now?'

'Now I know that whilst I may still be an idiot I'm not my father. I don't want to walk away from the baby. And I don't want to walk away from you.'

Another step and he was behind the sofa with her. Her only method of escape was to scramble over the back. The problem was flight was the very last thing on her mind.

Wait, Olivia. Don't just fall into his arms.

Adhering her feet to the floor, she turned to face him. 'But you will. You walked away from Charlotte.'

'Yes, I did. But I've done a lot of thinking these past weeks.' He rubbed the back of his neck. 'After Zeb and I parted ways years ago I was adrift.'

Against her will she felt her heart smite her as she imagined the incredible hurt of that rejection. So much worse than being rejected as an unknown baby.

'I thought a home would ground me,' he continued. 'Then I met Charlotte. She was an army child; she'd never had real roots. She was desperate for a home, as well. We were so caught up in the idea of having a home we thought that was what marriage was all about. We were in love with an idea, not each other.' His forehead creased into a frown of confusion. 'Does that make sense? Because it makes perfect sense to me now that I've met you and I've understood what love really is.'

'What *is* love?'

'It's wanting be with the person you love all the time. It's feeling able to share anything and not be judged. It's loving the sound of their voice and the smell of their hair.' His huge body was rigid with tension as he closed the gap further. 'I love you, Olivia. I know I messed up, but please believe this: I love you. And I will spend the rest of my life proving it to you and winning your love.'

Joy exploded in a firework of happiness, sending her giddy as she took the final steps so that she was standing close enough to touch him.

'You don't have to win my love, Adam.' She placed her hand on his heart. 'You already have it.'

'I do?' His smile was blinding in its radiance as he spanned her waist and tugged her closer.

'You do. I love you, Adam. I love how you make me feel beautiful and how you make me *want* to feel beautiful. For you. I love how I trust you to protect me and care for me. I love how you make me smoothies. I love the way you give and I love the way you take. I just love you. With all my heart. And all my other vital organs, too.'

She grinned at him.

'And I mean *all*! Turns out love isn't an illusion after all. It's wanting to be with someone and not caring where you are. If you don't want to live in a house then we'll live in a hotel suite. We can live in a tent, if you like.'

Adam shook his head. 'Liv, that week in Ko Lanta with you in that house was magical. I get that it was only a week, but not once did the walls so much as move. I want more of that. I want to go shopping and fill a house with clutter, with souvenirs of our life together. Which reminds me...' He dug into his jeans pocket and handed over a small tissue-wrapped packet before looping his arms back round her.

Olivia opened it up and gave a small gasp. Nestled in the folds were three silver charms.

Pushing her sleeve up, she unclasped the bracelet he'd given her. 'I'll put them on now.'

'A beer bottle to remind you of our first night together, a frangipani flower, and a ring.'

'A ring?' Olivia stilled.

Adam nodded and dug into his pocket again. He hauled in a breath and pulled out a velvet jewellery box. He popped it open and sank to one knee.

'Will you marry me, Liv?'

Tears of sheer joy dewed her eyelashes and thrills of bliss trembled though her as she nodded. 'Yes, Adam, I will. With all my heart.'

Her fingers quivered as he slid the exquisite diamond band on. Then she tugged him to his feet and a bubble of laughter escaped her lips. In her wildest dreams she'd never imagined that she, Olivia Evans, would be proposed to looking like this!

The grubby scarf still encased her hair, dust and grime smeared her face, and she was wearing a flowered apron that had seen better days. And she didn't give a stuff.

Secure in Adam's love for ever, she stepped forward into the warmth of his embrace and tilted her face up to receive a blissful kiss.

* * * * *

Mills & Boon® Hardback
August 2014

ROMANCE

Zarif's Convenient Queen	Lynne Graham
Uncovering Her Nine Month Secret	Jennie Lucas
His Forbidden Diamond	Susan Stephens
Undone by the Sultan's Touch	Caitlin Crews
The Argentinian's Demand	Cathy Williams
Taming the Notorious Sicilian	Michelle Smart
The Ultimate Seduction	Dani Collins
Billionaire's Secret	Chantelle Shaw
The Heat of the Night	Amy Andrews
The Morning After the Night Before	Nikki Logan
Here Comes the Bridesmaid	Avril Tremayne
How to Bag a Billionaire	Nina Milne
The Rebel and the Heiress	Michelle Douglas
Not Just a Convenient Marriage	Lucy Gordon
A Groom Worth Waiting For	Sophie Pembroke
Crown Prince, Pregnant Bride	Kate Hardy
Daring to Date Her Boss	Joanna Neil
A Doctor to Heal Her Heart	Annie Claydon

MEDICAL

Tempted by Her Boss	Scarlet Wilson
His Girl From Nowhere	Tina Beckett
Falling For Dr Dimitriou	Anne Fraser
Return of Dr Irresistible	Amalie Berlin

0714GEN STD HB

Mills & Boon® Large Print
August 2014

ROMANCE

A D'Angelo Like No Other	Carole Mortimer
Seduced by the Sultan	Sharon Kendrick
When Christakos Meets His Match	Abby Green
The Purest of Diamonds?	Susan Stephens
Secrets of a Bollywood Marriage	Susanna Carr
What the Greek's Money Can't Buy	Maya Blake
The Last Prince of Dahaar	Tara Pammi
The Secret Ingredient	Nina Harrington
Stolen Kiss From a Prince	Teresa Carpenter
Behind the Film Star's Smile	Kate Hardy
The Return of Mrs Jones	Jessica Gilmore

HISTORICAL

Unlacing Lady Thea	Louise Allen
The Wedding Ring Quest	Carla Kelly
London's Most Wanted Rake	Bronwyn Scott
Scandal at Greystone Manor	Mary Nichols
Rescued from Ruin	Georgie Lee

MEDICAL

Tempted by Dr Morales	Carol Marinelli
The Accidental Romeo	Carol Marinelli
The Honourable Army Doc	Emily Forbes
A Doctor to Remember	Joanna Neil
Melting the Ice Queen's Heart	Amy Ruttan
Resisting Her Ex's Touch	Amber McKenzie

Mills & Boon® Hardback
September 2014

ROMANCE

The Housekeeper's Awakening	Sharon Kendrick
More Precious than a Crown	Carol Marinelli
Captured by the Sheikh	Kate Hewitt
A Night in the Prince's Bed	Chantelle Shaw
Damaso Claims His Heir	Annie West
Changing Constantinou's Game	Jennifer Hayward
The Ultimate Revenge	Victoria Parker
Tycoon's Temptation	Trish Morey
The Party Dare	Anne Oliver
Sleeping with the Soldier	Charlotte Phillips
All's Fair in Lust & War	Amber Page
Dressed to Thrill	Bella Frances
Interview with a Tycoon	Cara Colter
Her Boss by Arrangement	Teresa Carpenter
In Her Rival's Arms	Alison Roberts
Frozen Heart, Melting Kiss	Ellie Darkins
After One Forbidden Night...	Amber McKenzie
Dr Perfect on Her Doorstep	Lucy Clark

MEDICAL

A Secret Shared...	Marion Lennox
Flirting with the Doc of Her Dreams	Janice Lynn
The Doctor Who Made Her Love Again	Susan Carlisle
The Maverick Who Ruled Her Heart	Susan Carlisle

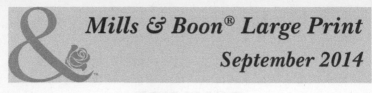

Mills & Boon® Large Print

September 2014

ROMANCE

The Only Woman to Defy Him	Carol Marinelli
Secrets of a Ruthless Tycoon	Cathy Williams
Gambling with the Crown	Lynn Raye Harris
The Forbidden Touch of Sanguardo	Julia James
One Night to Risk it All	Maisey Yates
A Clash with Cannavaro	Elizabeth Power
The Truth About De Campo	Jennifer Hayward
Expecting the Prince's Baby	Rebecca Winters
The Millionaire's Homecoming	Cara Colter
The Heir of the Castle	Scarlet Wilson
Twelve Hours of Temptation	Shoma Narayanan

HISTORICAL

Unwed and Unrepentant	Marguerite Kaye
Return of the Prodigal Gilvry	Ann Lethbridge
A Traitor's Touch	Helen Dickson
Yield to the Highlander	Terri Brisbin
Return of the Viking Warrior	Michelle Styles

MEDICAL

Waves of Temptation	Marion Lennox
Risk of a Lifetime	Caroline Anderson
To Play with Fire	Tina Beckett
The Dangers of Dating Dr Carvalho	Tina Beckett
Uncovering Her Secrets	Amalie Berlin
Unlocking the Doctor's Heart	Susanne Hampton

MILLS & BOON®

Why shop at millsandboon.co.uk?

Each year, thousands of romance readers find their
perfect read at millsandboon.co.uk. That's because
we're passionate about bringing you the very best
romantic fiction. Here are some of the advantages
of shopping at www.millsandboon.co.uk:

* **Get new books first**—you'll be able to buy your
  favourite books one month before they hit
  the shops

* **Get exclusive discounts**—you'll also be able to buy
  our specially created monthly collections, with up
  to 50% off the RRP

* **Find your favourite authors**—latest news,
  interviews and new releases for all your favourite
  authors and series on our website, plus ideas for
  what to try next

* **Join in**—once you've bought your favourite books,
  don't forget to register with us to rate, review and
  join in the discussions

Visit **www.millsandboon.co.uk**
for all this and more today!